My Own Voice

STILL LIFE WITH MEMORIES

VOLUME I

USA Today
Bestselling Author

UVI POZNANSKY

My Own Voice©2015 Uvi Poznansky

This novel can be read as a standalone novel, as well as a part of *Still Life with Memories*, a series describing events in the life of a unique family from multiple points of view.

Published by Uviart
P.O. Box 3233 Santa Monica CA 90408
Blog: uviart.blogspot.com
Email: uvi.author@gmail.com

First Edition 2015
Printed in the United States of America
Book design, cover design, and cover image by
Uvi Poznansky

Contents

Apart from Love

Chapter 1

Later, when I wake up, it takes me a while to grasp where I am, and even longer to figure out that I've lost time, that time has passed. The last thing I remember is like, making breakfast for him—and now, somehow, it's late afternoon.

I'm lying here on my side, with the bedside lamp shedding a dim light behind me. I can tell that his side of the bed is empty. Why am I here? How did I get here? Why am I so dazed, so confused? And where's Lenny?

I gaze across the ceiling and along the walls, trying to pick out every shade, every hint. And there, opposite the bed I spot my wedding dress which—now I recall—I've hung on the coat rack, right there in the corner.

The corner of the bedroom is the only place here which I reckon is truly mine. Strange, no? I still feel that way, despite having slept here with him, on and off, for like, the past ten years. I keep telling myself that I must claim this space, claim it as mine, right away. And maybe I will one day, when the baby's born.

I try to picture a crib here, next to me, and at once everything looks so much brighter. I hope the baby can soon feel something of what's in my heart—but not the confusion.

Staring at that corner I know one thing, and I know it real clear, at once: this lovely dress, made of heavy satin and trimmed with lace and beading and what not, which I've dyed, the morning after the wedding, orange at the top and purple at the bottom, so it can still be used in the future—like, at dances and parties and stuff—this dress isn't gonna fit me no more.

Up to now I've pictured it in my head, shining awful brilliant, just like a rainbow, and swirling all around me; and with every step, billowing between my legs, and like, making me adorable, so adorable in Lenny's eyes—but now that I touch my belly and feel the beginning, the very beginning of change, right here around my waist, what's the point of all that.

On the floor, under the hem of the dress, I can see two pairs of shoes: one is my new, white satin shoes, which Lenny's bought for me, like, two weeks ago, just for the wedding.

When he wants to, he can be real kind. He knows so well how to spoil a woman. He gave me a ring with a pink sapphire. I bet you it's real! Also, a gold chain with a locket, which at the last minute—like, just before saying, *I do*—I decided not to wear. I wanted to look classy, and worried that it's gonna be a bit much.

And the other pair? Now, that's my very first pair of high heel shoes. They're worn out, but still kinda bright, and chipped only a little. To this day I'm totally crazy about the color: hot pink!

Ten years ago I spotted them up there, in a store window, and for a whole month I stared at them every day, on my way home from school, and my heart sank, knowing I didn't have no money to buy them. I liked how the side of the strap was like, spruced up with a plastic rose, which has since fallen off. Awful cute, it was!

Then I found a job at this ice cream place, down there at the Santa Monica pier. I got my first week's pay, and was so happy, so thrilled to rush in and buy them, because they wasn't only pink—but glossy too, and because now I was just like an adult. Ma took one look at them and slapped me, which made me figure that now, I was gonna have no choice but to apply plenty of makeup, so that this side of my face, which was flaming red, won't stand out all that much.

Then she slapped me again, this time on the other side, which turned out to be just as stinging—but at least, it solved the problem for me, 'cause now I found myself, like, pretty even; you know, balanced on both sides.

Ma said I looked like a bitch in them shoes—but I didn't care, really I didn't, because it was my sixteenth birthday and it was my own damn money, for me to do as I please, and because I had to fight her, like, tooth and nail to keep the little I had, so that she won't take it from me, for my sake of course; and because most of all, I thought them shoes made me look just fine.

Now I can see one pink shoe standing lopsided, held up somehow in-between them white shoes; and the other pink one lying there, turned over, like some open-mouthed baby whale, trying to rise for a breath from a sea of dust.

Me, I still remember the first time I wore them, which was also the first time I met Lenny.

He was standing out there, on the other side of the pier. The lights on the Ferris Wheel had just started to come on. They was gleaming there, directly behind him.

Somehow I could spot his outline in the distance, in-between the swirly letters, which I couldn't read, because from the inside, which was where I was standing, left was right, right was left, flipped into looking kinda foreign, which can really confuse you.

3

But I knew them letters spelled the name of the place. They looked cool, too, like they're gonna drip and totally melt, floating up there on the pane of glass between us.

It was a hot summer evening, and the place was awful packed. I paced back and forth behind the counter, serving the customers, dishing out fresh smiles, scooping Dutch chocolate here and vanilla there, and trying to get a beat going, trying to sway my hips and at the same time, steady my step over my new, hot pink high heels, which isn't near as easy as you might think —at least, not on the first try.

After a while I noted that he started pacing just like me, back and forth, and with the same beat, too. I liked the bounce of his step. Right away I thought he was gonna make a fabulous dance partner. And I knew, really I did, it was gonna be a wild night.

You won't believe how wild it turned out to be—but in a different way than you might expect, like, an entirely different way. He was so handsome, too, with that slicked-back hair, just like them stars in the old movies!

And like, there was something about his walk, about the way he carried himself, that reminded me of Johnny, mom's previous boyfriend, the one who confessed to her that he couldn't get no respect from his wife.

Just like him, Lenny seemed to be in his early forties, and like, he was talking to himself from time to time. I bet he was rehearsing some excuse. Which made me bust out laughing, laughing so hard that my hat—that ice cream uniform hat, made of hard white paper folded in half—nearly flew off my pony tail. I mean, if you find yourself in such a bind, having to come up with one new story after another for the old wife, you might as well just get rid of her, and get yourself a new girl.

The minute our eyes met, I knew what to do: so I stopped in the middle of what I was doing, which was dusting off the glass shield over the ice cream buckets, and stacking up waffle cones here and sugar cones there. From the counter I grabbed a bunch of paper tissues, and bent all the way down, like, to pick something from the floor. Then with a swift, discrete shove, I stuffed the tissues into one side of my bra, then the other, 'cause I truly believe in having them two scoops—if you know what I mean—roundly and firmly in place.

Having a small chest is no good: men seem to like girls with boobs that bulge out. It seems to make an awful lot of difference, especially at first sight, which you can always tell by them customers, drooling.

I straightened up real fast, and it didn't take no time for him to come in. I was still serving another customer, some obnoxious woman with, like, three chins. She couldn't make up her mind if she wanted hot fudge on top or just candy sprinkles, and what kind, what flavor would you say goes well with pistachio nut, and how about them slivered almonds, because they do seem to be such a healthy choice, now really, don't they.

He came in and stood in line, real patient, right behind her. So now I noted his eyes, which was brown, and his high forehead and the crease, the faint crease right there, in the middle of it, which reminded me all of a sudden of my pa, who left us for good when I was only five, and I never saw him again —but still, from time to time, I think about him and I miss him so.

I could feel Lenny—whose name I didn't know yet—like, staring at me. It made me hot all over. For a minute there, I could swear he was gonna ask me how old I was—but he didn't.

And so, to avoid blushing, I turned to him and I said, boldly, "It's a crime?"

And he said, "What?"

And I said, "To be sixteen. It's a crime, you think?"

And he said, "Back in the days when I was young and handsome, that was no crime."

And I countered with, "Handsome you still are!"

He had no comeback for that, and me, I didn't have nothing with which I could follow it up. So I asked, "So? What kind of cone for you?" but that woman cut in, 'cause I was still holding her three-scoops tower of pistachio nut on a sugar cone. And she started to cry out, and like, demand some attention here, because hey, she was first in line and how about whipped cream? Or some of that shredded coconut?

So I smiled at her, in my most cool and polite manner, and squeezed out a big dollop of whipped cream, which was awesome, 'cause it calmed her down right away.

And I scattered some of them coconut flakes all over—quite a heap—and went even further, adding a cherry on top. At last, I raised the thing to my lips, because at this point, it was starting to drip already.

Then, winking at him, I passed my tongue over the top, and all around the ice cream at the rim of the cone, filling my whole mouth and, just to look sexy, also licking the tips of my fingers. Then I came around the counter, swaying my hips real pretty, and steadying myself over the wobbly high heels. I came right up to him, and before he could guess what kind of trouble I had cooked up in my head, I kissed him—so sweet and so long—on his lips, to the shouts and outcries of the offended customer.

The manager was like, outraged, not only because of this incident—but also because pink shoes wasn't allowed, no way no how, only black uniform shoes. She grabbed my ice cream hat, that thing made out of white paper, and pulled it right off my head, and threw it to the floor, smashing and crashing it. I was fired right there, on the spot.

He came out right away after me. I bet he figured it was his fault, 'cause it was over him that I've lost my job.

So he said, "Hi. My name is Lenny."

"Anita," I said, licking my lips, because they was still kinda sticky and tasted sweet, and because I think I look hot when my mouth has a shine.

It was getting awful dark already. And he said, like, "So, where do you live?"

And me, I figured that tonight, it would be good to hang out at home, 'cause ma was gonna be working late again.

We lived in the same one-bedroom place ever since I was five, when pa had paid the first month rent—but then he forgot, somehow, all about sending the second. Sometimes, things may fly right out of your mind. I totally get that.

Because of Santa Monica's rent control, the place was kinda cheap. Still, ma said that paying it was hard for her, 'cause without a high school diploma—which she never got, on account of never going to no high school—without that, no one wants you, and there is no way nowhere to get a decent, well-paying job.

For the last couple of years she worked as a cleaning lady by day and an unarmed security officer by night, both at the same place, a local clinic. Tonight, I figured, would be her night shift.

So when Lenny asked, "Would you like me to take you home?" I said, "Yes, take me."

"But," he said, "no more kissing, I mean it now. I do not want any trouble, and you are too young, you know, much too young for a man my age."

He had a fine way of talking, like no one else I knew. He talked, like, with such a clear cut enunciation. I'm awful proud of this word. It was from Lenny that I learned it. *Enunciation.* For my part, I could teach him a thing or two about *trouble.*

So later, while sticking the key in the door, I turned to him and said, "Trouble, that's my middle name," which was a line I used sometimes, 'cause it sounded so clever.

"No, really?" he said.

To which I replied by asking, "What, you think it's a crime? Like, kissing me, I mean?" And he said, "It's just... I do not want to start something which can lead nowhere, really."

What could I say to that, except, "There's no one home. Stay a minute. Is that a crime, too?"

I handed him an old record, something slow from the sixties, which years ago used to bring tears to ma's eyes, because—in spite of looking so tough—she still had a soft spot somewhere in her, even if most of the time you can't find it. She used to play it often—but now not so much no more.

So I thought he might like it. Lenny put it on the record player, so in a second the mood was better, even though the thing squeaked from time to time.

He turned to me the minute I untied my pony tail, and told me I reminded him of a girl he used to know, and would I like to dance.

I stepped out of my shoes and into his arms, and before he could say anything I slipped out of my dress, too. I thought I looked, like, a little too slender in my panties, so I told him to close his eyes—but at this point, because of being so aroused, and trying so hard not to show it, I forgot all about them tissues at each side of my bra, which now and again, made a slight swoosh.

Later I wondered if he wondered about that.

I rose to the tips of my toes, feeling the touch of his shirt and the pleat of his pants, right against my bare skin. And I placed my hands on his shoulders, and felt his hands on my hips.

And so he held me there, a long, long time in the dark. And me, I got to touch his lips, and that crease up there, on his forehead, and we swayed back and forth: I clinging to him, he— to that one girl, the girl he used to know.

Then he moved away abruptly, saying that he was too old for me, and anyway, what was he doing, he had a child, a boy just a year older than me. So I took a step closer, like, to close the gap again. And feeling lost, like a stray kitten out in the cold, I said, "Just hold me, Lenny. Just hold me tight. I need you so bad."

And the minute I said it, I knew he needed to hear these words, needed to know that he was really needed.

After a while I whispered, like, "Just say something to me. Anything." And I thought, Any other word apart from *love*, 'cause that word is diluted, and no one knows what it really means, anyway. Then he kissed me—even without the ice cream —and said my name, like, he tasted it in his mouth, and rolled it on his tongue, which made me awful happy. And we started our dance again:

I came as he backed away, and then in reverse, I backed away as he came, and we came and went, went and came this way for a long while until, all of a sudden, the front door opened and there was ma, standing there with a new boyfriend this time, a guy whose name I didn't even know.

She opened her fist—I could hear the bong of the key chain as it dropped to the floor—and before she could slap me, I ran as fast and as far as my legs could take me, right out the door.

Then, yelling *Bitch* at the top of her voice, ma picked up my dress, which had been left there, in the middle of the floor, and threw it. She threw it flying down the staircase after me—but for some reason, them pink shoes stayed behind.

They stayed until the next day, when Lenny went there for me, to get some of my stuff. Perhaps he figured he was in charge of me now, and so he paid for a motel room, and went on paying it, 'cause it was on his account that I lost my job and the roof over my head, both on the same night.

Who's there? What was that, just now?

I can feel, like, a slight breath behind me. I can hear the click of the knob, on the bedside lamp up there, over my shoulder. It's made the light stronger, and the shadows—sharper. I need to know who it is—but at this point, I don't barely feel like turning around.

And I can't decide if this is so because I'm still pretty dazed, or because lying here on my side feels better, so much better for the cramps. I bet I can figure who it is simply by spotting the reflections, right there in the mirror.

It's a freestanding mirror, tilted over its feet, set in an ornate oval frame, which is so classy, and like, fit for a queen, and which used to be hers. I mean, his ex-wife. But then, just the thought of it—I mean, the thought of catching sight of myself in *her* mirror—is like, strange. It gives me goosebumps.

And it isn't just old wives' tales, or just my nerves. I've seen images of Natasha. Lenny keeps them old pictures stashed away in the drawer, next to his side of the bed, and—like, quite by chance—I found them one day. If not for the age spots spreading over the pictures, and if not for the yellowing, you could swear that face is mine.

So whenever I find myself passing there, by that mirror, I close my eyes, or turn my head away. And I ask myself then, What on earth did he find in me—a simple girl, with no high school diploma, who at times can't help but making him bored stiff?

What did he need me for—me and my lousy *enunciation*—when he had already married this woman who, by everything I've learned about her, was so fine and so talented, and came from an awful long line of musicians?

And why, why did he tell me, that first time we danced, that I reminded him of a girl he used to know?

Lying here, in what used to be *her* side of the bed—a side which isn't mine, at least not yet—I'm thinking about her, worrying, like, Is she gonna come back here, any time soon, to claim her place?

The other day, standing there behind the kitchen door, I could hear Lenny. He lowered his voice when he told his son that yes, she'd been there, in the hospital, visiting him. And I think he said that he'd shut his eyes, just to be focused, to feel her; which is a bad sign for me.

I'm wondering now how much time I've lost, and where Lenny might be, 'cause if not for his injuries, and being stuck now in a wheelchair, I can picture him in my head real easy, pacing back and forth somewhere else right now.

It Is Not Too Late

Chapter 2

I can hear a noise of some kind, clicking awful close to my ear, on the other side, I mean, Lenny's side of the bed. I try to stay still, because of this dull pain, and because of wondering if, somewhere deep inside, my baby can feel it, too.

Then I turn my head—just a little—and take a peak over my shoulder. I glance real quick at that standalone mirror, which is facing away from me. And what do I see reflected there, if not something that's, like, so strange to my eyes, so unusual, that it makes me want to blink, or wipe them in awe.

Three squares of fuzzy wool are being held there, suspended in midair. Directly behind them hang three shadows, under which you can see three chubby old women, crinkling their noses—long, longer, longest. They're straining their crossed, beady eyes with great focus, under three pairs of glasses, and clinking, clinking, clinking three pairs of knitting needles, like, all together now!

And there, on the floor, you can see three balls of thick yarn chasing each other, and from time to time, getting tied in knots, every which way across them fat ankles.

Anyway, at first glance them old women look kinda similar, like a rough, wrinkled copy of each other, what with those high arched, strange eyebrows. I pinch myself, but they're still there—in the mirror as well as outside of it—no matter how long I try blinking and wiping my eyes. It takes me a while to tell them apart:

The one sitting to the left, she's toothless. The one in the middle has a pimple on her veined temple. And the one to the right, well, her nose isn't only the longest, but also the knobbiest of all three.

Wrapped around her neck is a long tape measure, the edges of which roll all the way down and curl there, in her lap, next to a pair of scissors.

All of a sudden, like something has clicked in my head, I know who she is: this is Hadassa Rosenblatt, known to all as aunt Hadassa—though nobody can tell me exactly whose aunt she is anyway—she was the one spreading nasty, awful rumors about me, saying I was dating some other boyfriend, like, behind Lenny's back.

At the time, I decided to make things real easy for her, and told her there's no need for her to come to my wedding, and in fact it would be so much better if she'd stay as far as she could from me; which made her sisters, Frida and Fruma, stay home, too. Since then, my mind is kinda at ease—except for wondering, Why the gossip? Why did she try meddling in my affairs? And now, ain't them three sisters gonna curse me, like witches do, in old children stories?

And what on earth they been doing here, in my bedroom, sitting behind me, watching me so quiet—so mute like, even—that for the last hour I didn't hear no squeak out of them? Or else was it me, was I too sleepy, too dazed to notice them?

In a blink of an eye I can tell that aunt Hadassa can tell, somehow, that I'm awake, and that I've been watching her for the last few minutes.

So at once, she straightens her back and elbows aunt Frida, who in turn elbows aunt Fruma. And they all nod a slight nod to each other, and each sister in her turn pulls some yarn from her ball and then kicks it, so it goes into a whirl and then settles there, at their feet. All of which seems so smooth, so precise, so much like a chorus line; which reminds me what Lenny told me about their past.

I remember, he said that one of these days, he'd like to finish his story about them, which goes something like this:

Having fled from Poland during World War II, the three Rosenblatt sisters arrived in Paris, where they discovered glamor, or at least the chance for it.

They bleached their hair super blond, so as to put the shtetl, and the horrors they must have suffered, right out of their mind, along with the old way of life.

Around the same time, they changed their names to Brigitte, Monique, and Veronique. Along with their names, they threw out a few other things which had failed to serve them: their long, dark skirts, and their modesty.

Wearing frilly underwear and black stockings, they auditioned for a show at a nightclub, a highly acclaimed nightclub called the Folies Bergère—only to be rejected, because sadly, their dance routine was too nice and conservative; which made them furious, and even more driven to make it.

So with clenched teeth, they learned how to lift their skirts, and flap them about in a highly erotic, flirtatious manner. After several months of hard, painstaking work, the three sisters finally became an overnight sensation.

They ended up joining a cheaply produced show in the nightclub district of Montmartre. Their fame spread. They became known for their fancy cancan costumes, which left them practically naked.

Their earlier, orthodox upbringing didn't seem to inhibit them in the least. Behind the curtains, they went from one scandal to the next, and had countless affairs.

They never married, or had children. Later, in secret, they told Natasha that at one time Brigitte—also known as Hadassa—had gone through a difficult abortion. She couldn't afford a real doctor, so who knows what instrument was used there.

Soon after, she'd been kicked out from the show, because sadly, she couldn't perform the required cartwheel any more, or even the high kicks.

All this is, like, awesome! But me, I find it hard to believe that there was a time when aunt Hadassa could do any of that. To this day, she still wears the black stockings, as do her sisters, and she can keep a beat, an incredibly fast beat, which you can hear by the clicking of her needles. Anyway, she's declined with age. Her flesh looks doughy, and she's kinda heavy.

Looking at her makes me decide one thing right away: I'm never gonna grow old! I simply refuse to do that.

Lenny tells me that later, when they moved to the States and settled in Los Angeles, the Rosenblatt sisters became very close to his wife. They adore Natasha, perhaps because of having no kids of their own; which in the end, comes down to hating me.

Of one thing I'm sure: if they could wave a magic wand, or a needle or something, to undo whatever binds us, Lenny and me, to each other—this marriage and above all, this pregnancy—they would do so without thinking twice.

What's more, they seem to keep a secret among them, when it comes to this question: where's Natasha? She hasn't shown up here for the last, say, five years; which is cool with me—but still, strange.

If I ask them about it, which I did at one time, the sisters would find a way to skirt the question. And if I ask Lenny, he would hide the truth, somehow, with a kiss, and anyway, he won't give me no real answer, either.

All of a sudden aunt Hadassa clears her throat and says, "Nu? Why are you staring at my eyebrows?"

To which I say, "Who, me?"

"Oy, dear! When you're older, you'll understand," she says; which serves only one purpose: to inflame me.

And so I ask, "Understand what?"

Aunt Hadassa wraps the yarn onto the left needle, and loops it around. "Understand this, Anita," she says. "The thing about eyebrows: it is the first thing to go, when you get older."

Me, I don't have nothing to add to this piece of wisdom, to which she adds, "They hang down, I mean, heavily, over your eyes, and show your age, being so droopy and white, and so slick, to the point of resisting any fix, any type of makeup."

"I'm never gonna grow old," I state.

Which makes her curl her lips, like she knows something I don't. "Give it time, dear, give it time! My, my, Anita, you'll end up just like me, having to pluck them! Pluck-pluck-pluck! And then, just so you can look halfway presentable, paint them right back in, dear—as best you can."

"Really," I insist. "It isn't your eyebrows. It's that nose on you. That's the thing that fascinates me."

Naturally she seems surprised to hear that; which forces me to clarify, "I really, really hate it."

"So do I," she admits, for no other reason than to try to appease me.

Now aunt Hadassa slides the knot onto the other needle, and so does aunt Frida, and aunt Fruma too, in her turn. Their arms seem pretty wrinkled, like yesterday's newspaper.

I lift my pinkie finger and tilt it ever so slightly, as if holding a teacup.

"Hey, aunt Hadassa," I call. "See here, my hand?"

"What about it?" says she.

Now waving my fist in the air, I say, "I just want you to know that if you ever stick your nose, like, anywhere close to me, or to any of my private affairs, you're gonna leave me no choice, see, but to punch it. Seriously, that's one thing I learned from my ma, and I warn you now: I learned it real good."

"Ha," she puffs. "Your affairs, they seem to stick out like a sore thumb, and right in our noses, too. It is you who, by fainting at the most ill-advised time, forced this stink on us, on our delicate sensibilities."

"Why, how d'you mean?" I ask, totally confused.

"Who do you think has been taking care of you all day," she says, "Ha, princess?" And aunt Frida joins in, "Who has been wiping the dribble from the corner of your mouth?" This, while aunt Fruma chimes in, "And who, do you suppose, has been changing that pad, down in your cute little panties?"

"What?" I ask, in great outrage.

"Yes, dear," says aunt Hadassa. "Lenny, he found you right there, right outside the kitchen door. He said he'd called you, and called you again, then again, because the omelette, it was almost ready, and you never answered. So he figured you must have left."

"And the omelette," she continues, before I have time to catch my breath. "Oy, it was getting cold, and of course it is no good cold, so finally he figured, of course, that he was hungry, because all he had for breakfast was coffee. You know he is sick of your egg salad, right? He never eats it, dear, now does he. Why you keep making it is beyond me!"

By now I've opened my mouth to answer, which at once makes her raise her voice. "So," she says, "he transferred the omelette to a plate, and added some butter on top, and waited a bit, just to let it melt, and to make sure you, dear, were not coming back. Nu, then he just ate it, after which he came out and realized, all of a sudden, that quite sadly, he had been mistaken; that in fact, you were there all along, in the corridor, lying flat on your back, and barely breathing, too. Which is when he picked up the phone and, finally, called us for help."

In disbelief I say, "Help? I don't need none of your help! And where, where is he now?"

To which she says, "My, my! He is so exhausted now, after all that excitement, I mean the wedding first of all, and then his stay at the hospital. Too weak, I am afraid, to be of any use! And his son, Ben, nu! What can I say? Men! They managed to lift you, somehow, and carry you to bed. So now, consider yourself lucky, dear, to be in one piece. As soon as we came, they went out."

"Out? Out where?" I ask.

But in place of an answer she just waves her hand, saying, "I do not wish to lump them all in one heap, but somehow, you see, men can never take care of themselves, let alone take care of us women. They are never there for us when we need them—now are they!"

For a minute I hesitate to ask, "What did you say, just now, about changing my pad? What pad?"

Which makes her lay down her square of wool and say, this time real slow and careful, "You know you are bleeding, right?"

It is then that I try to jump from the bed, because not only do I feel ashamed, even violated, which of course isn't the first time in my life—but all of a sudden I sense a cramp, just like a stab, down in my stomach, in the same place where so far, the pain's been dull.

So she hurries over, and places the palm of her hand, like, real heavy, on top of my shoulder. "You can't do that, dear," she says, pushing me back, and propping up my pillow—even as I rise up to ask, "Why? Why the hell not?"

"Nu," she says. "Just be a good girl for me and lie down, nice and easy now, and for God's sake, be still. Take up knitting if you like. I can bring you instructions," she adds, "for anything. Baby blanket? Baby socks? Just tell me, dear, tell me what you like."

Despite her offer, I'm sick of the way she keeps saying *dear*.

There's no way for me to know what she means by that, because her tone is like, bitter, and it don't hardly agree with the sweet taste of this word, and because she keeps repeating it all too often; all of which tells me one thing: aunt Hadassa is torn. She can't decide between wishing me ill—and helping me back to my feet.

"I won't lie down," I say, defiantly. "And I really, really don't like knitting."

Her painted eyebrows arch even higher, and I begin to get an uneasy feeling, because at this point, she's much too close to me, and the light bounces off her needle much too sharply, and now the tip is right here, against my skin, and it scratches.

I point a finger at her, like, right in her face, to make her take note of my nails. "Shove off! Away from me," I tell her. "I mean it, don't you dare come any closer to me with them fine needles."

"I see," says aunt Hadassa.

She wraps the yarn around her index finger and plucks it, as if to transmit a message by wire. "A feisty little kitten," she says, "are you now!" At which time aunt Frida asks, "She's a kitten?" and aunt Fruma confirms, "Yes: a feisty little one!"

By now Aunt Hadassa has stepped back, and with a tight-lipped expression she sits there and starts sewing the three squares of wool together, using some fancy sort of a stitch, and clicking her tongue, and sighing, like, "My, my."

After doing this for a while, she pushes them glasses up her nose, and raises her eyes to me and says, "I'm trying to talk to you, dear, like I was your ma, you know."

To which I say, "And what makes you think I need another ma? One's more than enough! And you, you don't know nothing about my ma."

"I guess I don't," she has to admit. "But being pregnant is not for sissies, dear. You must make sure you are strong, like me."

At hearing this, I can't hide my disgust. "If this is what strength looks like, I swear, I'm gonna take disease."

"I see," says she. "In that case, it's not too late, you know."

And before I can ask, "What is?" she goes on to drive the point home.

"I have done it before, and it can make things so much easier for you, because really, you like to run around and have your fun, don't you. And here you are, poor dear, lying in bed, confined, probably, for weeks, if not months. Now with all this bleeding going on, my, my, who knows what has happened there."

She points her needle at me, stressing, "Maybe it's no good anyway, I mean, not viable, if you know what I am saying—"

"Don't—don't you dare say it," I flash a warning at her. "For God's sake, bite your tongue!"

At that minute, aunt Hadassa picks up the scissors; which is when I suddenly remember that piece of music which I heard with Lenny.

He took me to some opera, Wagner I think, which was long and kinda difficult to get, but he told me to listen, and he explained it all to me, and from there I remember them, the three Norns: They spun the thread of fate, and they sang, like, the song of the future.

Beware, they sang.

Beware, I tell myself now, as aunt Hadassa holds up the yarn, and snips it.

And with a sigh she leans into her feet and gets up. So do her sisters, and all their images in that oval, standalone mirror, right there in the opposite corner.

"Nu, we are going to leave now," she says. "We are going to hurry out, dear, because we do not want you to tell us we should go. Just think about it, will you? I was just saying... It is not too late, really... You are in pain, dear, I can see it quite plainly. And there is still time to end this."

The three sisters file out with a quick, matching step, and go out to the corridor, followed closely by a whirl in the air, in which you can spot three bounces—high, higher, highest—of three balls of yarn.

And as they make their final exit, I shout at them as loud as I can, despite that sharp pain right here, in my guts, "Aunt Hadassa!"

I hear them stopping in their tracks out there, behind that door.

"What is it," whispers one. "What does she want," whispers another. And the last one answers, probably with a wave of a hand, "Who knows... Maybe, just to meow a little."

Which in turn, makes me roar, "Who needs you! You, who think you can tell me what to do, and what not to do, and whether or not my pregnancy is like, viable, and should it come to full term, or not! I just wish that you leave me alone! Get the hell out! Get out of my womb, where it is not your business to be! And if I don't see none of you never again, it's gonna be too soon!"

A Promise, Aborted

Chapter 3

For a while I leaf through this book, which Lenny's bought me. I bet he's real excited. He so looks forward to becoming a father, the second time around. I can just see him in my head, like, holding the baby's hand, guiding him already in his first steps. Then, letting go, he's gonna take a step or two back, and hold his breath, waiting there for the little one to walk into his open arms.

Lenny's gonna buy him a brand new tricycle, and teach him how to set his little feet on top of them pedals, and push, push harder, even harder—yeah! Just so! And again: Go on, push, until—oh boy! With great joy, he's gonna clap his hands, because here—for the first time—you could detect a move, a slight move ahead.

And then, a few years down the road, he's gonna surprise our child with a large, shining bicycle, and adjust the training wheels as time goes by, until they wasn't needed no more; at which point, Lenny would remove them, and hold them in his hands, like, to weigh them for a moment, and try to wipe the rust, and wish that time would like, slow down, just a little, because it's hard, so hard for the old heart to let go.

Yes, Lenny needs a son: someone to need him, trust him, and make him trust himself again.

I turn the page over, only to find some of them words much too long—but I read them anyway and like, I *enunciate* them, as slowly and as clearly as I can, 'cause it's gonna make him proud of me, and make me worthy of him.

The book says that just four weeks after *conception*, basic facial features will begin to appear, including *passageways*, I repeat, passageways that will make up the inner ear, and arches that will *contribute*, contribute, I say aloud, to the jaw. And it says that the baby may now be a quarter of an inch long, which sounds like they're talking about some lizard, or maybe a fish.

But the book don't say nothing about what I'm really worried about, which is: how to become a ma—and at the same time, how to be totally different from my ma.

Me, I often wonder about that, 'cause it's kinda hard to know the right thing to do, even with the best of intentions, when all you have before you is nothing, nothing but a life cursed by violence, and by misery, and by a long list of mistakes.

Like the time when I was fourteen, and ma called me *Bitch*, for no better reason than me telling her that, like, I'd missed my period. I wasn't sure if she called me that because I was pregnant—or because she didn't want to hear it.

At any rate, ma pondered the *situation*. This was what she called it back then, a situation. And she gave me a smack across my face when she figured it was Johnny's baby, which was real bad, not only because he was already married—but because he was also dating her at the time. And if there was one thing she hated, it was the idea of sharing.

After the blow I could taste blood in my mouth. And when I touched it with my tongue, one of my teeth felt kinda loose, and after a while it started to rock back and forth.

Once she simmered down, ma said, "There's still time. It's not too late."

And she took me to that clinic, where she'd just joined the cleaning staff. And they did her a personal favor, so that instead of paying a full charge, she could put in some extra hours, like, for a few months. And there, they took care of the *situation*, but not of the tooth.

And so, I ended up losing it.

Me, I'm awful lucky, 'cause you can't tell it's missing—unless I'm having real good fun and busting out laughing, which sometimes makes me forget to keep my mouth shut.

But right now I have to bite my lips.

Either that, or dig my nails, like, deep into the flesh of my hand, so that them cramps, they're gonna stop, or at least fade away. So I close the book, reach over to the bedside lamp, and click its knob.

And at once, the place has changed. All these fancy pieces of furniture, and this entire bedroom, in which I don't really belong, with its walls—those here around me and those over there, beyond the threshold, out in a corridor—all of these things ain't solid no more. In a blink, they've lost their bright, yellow sides as well as their opposite, dark sides.

There ain't no contrasts anymore, so that now, you can't define no objects as, say, a four poster bed, or a coat hanger in a corner, or a wooden headboard, part of which is reflected there, in that mirror.

And instead, the whole space has become kinda fluid, like a gray, smoky swamp, given to the wild storm in my head, in which a shard here, a shard there start floating, in a total muddle.

And I ain't even sure if them shards are, like, in the shape of things that have already taken place, or the shape of things yet to come—but somehow I know that from now on, no matter what happens, I ain't alone: There's new life in me.

I touch myself under the blanket, brushing my fingers real slow, from the navel up to the crease right here, under my chest, which is where I can feel the change: My breasts, they've grown so much firmer than before, and my nipples, they've gotten so much larger, like a drop turning into a ripple.

I let my hand hover over the place where I imagine my baby, and picture in my head how them things, them passageways start to form, connecting like, by magic, from here to there, forging little nerves in all the right places inside this tiny creature, all quarter inch of him.

The two of us feel this bond, this warmth right here, coming across the thin gap between the skin of my belly and the skin of the palm of my hand. And so, we're happy. And then, then I stop to breathe—I gasp—I breathe deeper, deeper, so I can take it, take the pain.

Which in a flash, brings back to me that which I want to forget. It's the memory of that clinic, where they took care of the *situation*, and of how I came to, in that horrible place, and found myself lying there, flat on my back, feeling wounded.

Immobile, I stared for a long while at some blurry sort of a border, which gave a cold, metallic shine, not getting at first that it came from the rail, the side rail of the bed, which was raised, like, well above the level of my head.

So even without thinking—or knowing where I was—I felt like an animal, trapped.

Trying to come out of this state of paralysis, I started to notice a slight noise, 'cause them coil springs, they was creaking under me, which sounded almost like a sigh. There was mist in my head, and I tried to clear it, tried to focus.

The bed was awful high, so even if I could somehow gather my strength and take hold of the rail, even if I could lower the thing and then, swing my legs right there, over the edge—still, I wasn't sure if my feet could reach down, all the way to the floor.

All the while, there was a sound, a sharp sound breaking through to me. Someone out there, someone I couldn't even see was screaming, screaming real wild, like a kid scared out of her wits, crying for help with no clear words, and without ever stopping.

The ceiling loomed over my head, and the floor was white and shiny, and a smell rose from it, a pungent smell of some cleaning detergent. Me, I looked around me, and now I could see that the room had several other hospital beds, all of which seemed as shaky, and as high as the one in which I was trapped, on account of being set, somehow, on wheels.

I could make out some outlines, white outlines of bodies on white sheets. A few stretched flat on their backs; others, like, curled in the shape of a question mark.

Them women, I gathered, they was just like me: having a situation, and letting someone take care of it for them, and trying to forget, and heal from that which, like ma said, had to be done.

All of them seemed to be caged, much like me. Their faces was washed out, their expressions—numb. They was just knocked, like, out of their senses.

Looking at them I became kinda curious. I asked myself, who was the one screaming, 'cause they all seemed to be so sleepy, so eerily quiet, even though from time to time you could see a head turning, or a hand lifting or falling.

And me, I even became angry, madly angry at that unseen woman, whose voice pierced me. She roared, arousing something in my heart which was so annoying, so alarming, so crazed even—until at last I thought, Enough! Just shut the hell up! Why isn't nothing being done here, I mean like, anything to silence her! Slap the madwoman! Restrain her! Strap her in a straightjacket! This is a clinic, after all! Tie her up, so she can't stir up trouble no more!

And on that note, all of a sudden it came to me: somehow I knew, right then, that she was no other—no one else but me.

And still unable to stop myself from wailing, I began to listen, I mean, really listen to my own voice. I tried to take apart the different notes flying—with such force, such anguish—out of my throat.

I could hear different breaths, different speech sounds. Some was like, open, some—blocked. Finally I made a complete sense of it all. It was then that at last, I got it.

"Ma," I heard me raving, on and on and on, "Ma, take me, take me from here, take me, ma, please! Take me before it is too late!"

Little by little I regained control over myself. And the voice—my voice—which by now was like, hoarse from shouting, became softer and softer still, until, at last, it faded away.

I laid there exhausted, trying to catch my breath, asking myself, When would she come? When would she take me back, take me home?

And I knew right then that I won't never be quite the same. This was the day that changed me. From now on, my life would be measured not by a stretch of years, my fourteen years—but by the depth of this pain, this sorrow.

So I asked myself, What could I bring back, what would I remember out of it?

With some effort I recalled being led into the operation room, trembling a little in that skimpy paper gown, being told to mount the bed, and like, feeling them fingers—so cold on my outstretched arm—as the nurse had tried, several times, to find my vein.

But then, after that I couldn't recall nothing, nothing but that screaming, that goddam earsplitting screaming in my head. Thank God that was over.

I went back in my head, searching for an earlier moment, the moment I'd stopped in front of the entrance door, shedding tears, even kicking the stairs and pounding the wall with my fist, refusing to go into that clinic. I recalled arguing with ma, pleading with her to let me go, let me turn back, 'cause it was a school day, and I shouldn't miss it, really.

But she insisted that what I shouldn't miss was my future, because it was no good for me to repeat her mistakes, and if I did better in school, and scored better grades, especially in math, and learned, at long last, how to subtract my age from hers, I would know just exactly what she meant.

At any rate, keeping the baby was out of the question, 'cause it would, like, screw up my entire life. After all, she said, I was still a little girl myself, and despite thinking myself a woman I knew nothing, really, absolutely not a thing about parenting. And what's more, I didn't have no partner, no man with whom I could share the burden.

And by *burden* she meant, raising a child; which made me feel awkward, and like a burden myself.

At last I found myself having to obey her, because like, part of me reckoned she meant well, and she was right, too. And anyway, as everyone says, ma knows best—even though she went on dating Johnny for a whole month after that.

But the other part of me recoiled in fear at the thought, the mere thought of entering that door. I didn't want no procedure, 'cause I wanted so bad to hold on to the baby. In spite of everything ma had just said, I believed I was, like, destined to have him. Me, I could see, yes, I could just picture what lied ahead.

My little one would gurgle and coo right here, in my arms. I would be brushing my lips over his scalp—ever so gentle—careful not to touch nowhere close to the tender spot, right there at the top. I could almost feel the fine fuzz of his hair, real soft, tickling my cheek.

In my head I could kiss, I could almost swallow his tiny fingers. They would wrap around my finger, their nails so pink, so incredibly clear. And the little hands, they would stroke my hair or like, search for my breast.

Then I would touch the nipple to my baby's lips, and watch him latch on and like, suck, suck, swallow, breathe; suck, suck, swallow, breathe.

All the while his eyes would be fixed on me, curious to see, to separate my face out of that blurry chaos, that first, misty sight of lights and of shadows. And so I promised myself: I would give him that which I never got. I would become such a good mama, like no mama ever was! I would keep him safe right here, close to my heart.

The loss of this hope, that was the thing that was so painful. I couldn't hold it back, my grief. It came like, rushing, bursting out of me as I was lying there—even before I awoke, before I took full control of my body, or regained my spirit. It came out with every breath, every roar as it blasted off, soaring into the air above me. The roar of a wounded tigress.

This was the Anita whose voice I heard, for the first time in my life, that day twelve years ago.

Because who the hell cares? Who cares, really, if *there's still time*, and who cares if *it's not too late*, when your arms is empty. Who cares about the future, when your destiny is lost, and your promise—aborted, and by God, there's no way, no way no more to undo the damage.

A girl, a wild girl with green, kittenish eyes, that's how most people see me in their head, how they choose to fancy me. But then, who're they to decide? Can they hear what's inside, in my head? Me, I know different. There's a voice, there's a roar of a tigress in me, like, a fierce mama tigress, ready to leap into action and do anything, anything to protect her cub.

Beware, because this, you see, is the Anita I am today.

Keeper of Secrets

Chapter 4

The bleeding was real bad last night, and there wasn't no one there I could call for help—or so I thought. I've managed to slip off the bed, and go wandering around the apartment, supporting myself, somehow, along the walls.

I get myself a drink of water. At first, all's black around me— except for the two luminous tips, which mark the hands of the alarm clock down there, in the hall.

Me, I can't hear no breathing and no snoring nowhere in this place, which makes me shudder, shudder at the thought that what I've feared all along is happening, perhaps, right at this moment: I'm trouble, I mean, too much trouble for him, so Lenny must have gone. He's left me here, so now I'm all alone in this place. Abandoned.

Them blinds, they're flapping, beating against each other in the breeze, down there across the sliding glass door, which is slightly open, and lets some cold air into the living room. And sneaking in, between one blind and another, come thin streaks of moonlight, which fill me with fear.

They look just like swords, advancing stealthily across the floor, giving a sudden, silvery flash when you least expect it, and like, aiming their blades at that hateful, monstrous thing, which seems so much bigger in the dark: her piano.

I drag myself away from the light of the moon. Exhausted, I flop onto the bench. I stare at the polished top of the piano, which seems to radiate from the shadows, and where, I know, there's a long, twisty scratch. For sure Lenny blames me for it. He's cross with me, most of the time. And I bet he won't never forgive me, on account of that mistake, which I made nearly three weeks ago, at the wedding:

I should've kicked off my high heels, or at least, pointed them away, so they would hover, like, just above the surface, when—in front of everyone—I laid myself down on top of the damn thing.

And maybe it wasn't a mistake exactly, 'cause for Lenny, the piano is so much more than a musical instrument, which makes me hate it. I really do. Me, I can't exactly explain it—but like, I wish it would disappear, or break down, or something.

I remember the first morning I spent here, in this apartment, a month after his wife had left him. I sat down right here, on this bench in front of her piano, which looked whiter than white, because it was displayed against the background of a silvery blue wallpaper, which buckled at the seams, here and there.

With great caution I brushed my fingers lightly across them keys. And from the belly of the beast a sound came, shaking the air, a soft, low grumble ending with a hum; which startled me.

Facing me was her notebook, with a beautiful signature, which had plenty of twists and turns across the cover, and which was kinda hard to read—but at last I could make it out as *Natasha*. Next to the notebook was an old picture of her. I could see right away that she could easily be mistaken for my sister: her face was just like mine, and so was the red hair.

A majestic bust—the bust of Beethoven—perched above me. At the time I didn't hardly know who or what Beethoven was.

Anyhow, I was so scared that it made my hair curl. The bust seemed to gaze fiercely at the air with them marble eyes, eyes as intense as they was vacant. I turned around and could see Lenny, right there on the sofa, looking at me strange like, as if he was seeing some ghost.

He came over and sat down on the bench right here, beside me, and turned the photograph over, to hide his wife from me and perhaps, from himself. I thought he would put his arm around me, so we could start kissing—but instead, he took a long time to explain about them keys, and studied my fingers carefully, which made me feel awkward, and sorry, too. Sorry that my fingers wasn't longer, and sorry that I couldn't spread them apart no wider, the way Natasha could, being a pianist.

I was real sorry that my thumb looked kinda thick, which meant I was a simple, earthy girl. This, according to my ma. She ought to know: years ago—before being hired as a cleaning lady —ma had worked in Venice Beach, down at the boardwalk, as a fortune teller.

I remember her eyes. They looked downright stunning under the false eyelashes. As part of her gig, she would read the palm of my hand and like, shake her head with great concern for my future, so the hoop earrings would tinkle, as would the beaded necklaces and the jangle bracelets. Then her fake crystal ball would light up, at which time she would take firm hold of my hand and like, raise it up inside her fist, to show the crowd gathering around us how my thumb looked, how stubby it was, and how my lifeline, there on the palm of my hand, had an unusual, split end.

This scared me, really—because me, I was only seven years old back then—and it made some of the onlookers drop their jaws, like, in great awe.

They would come even closer, and press around us, eager to gain some insight into their own fate, and into each line on their palms and each little mark, and what all of them things could possibly mean. For a good price, ma would give out advice— mixed in with some warnings—which she crafted, like, in vague, immensely puzzling phrases.

But then, she didn't explain what the trouble was, exactly, with the split end of my lifeline; which left me kinda wondering. For sure ma couldn't tell, back then, that I would hook up with someone like Lenny: a married man who had a son a year older than me.

Now, in spite of sitting right next to me, Lenny didn't notice no problem with the shape of my thumbs; which was lucky, 'cause he raised his eyes for a second to the bust of Beethoven, and then, with a sudden spunk, like he was about to take a long, difficult leap, asked me if I wanted to learn how to play music.

And I said yes, 'cause I was sixteen, going on seventeen, and so I hoped that my hands could still grow a little, and maybe with some practice, my fingers could kinda stretch out, and become as long and as nimble as Natasha's. And then, perhaps, he would stop comparing us to each other all the time in his head, and—to my relief—he would give up trying to mold me, like, in her shape.

Let me be me, Lenny. Just let me be who I am.

During the next few days, I toyed with the idea of enrolling in a Beginning Piano class in Santa Monica College. Lenny was real eager about it, and he even paid the tuition fee for me, and promised it was gonna open me up to a world of wonder, and inspire me, and teach me about them notes, and about rhythm, chords, and pedaling, and how to apply them basics to classical music.

But then, a few weeks later, when I came back from the first class session, he changed his tune, perhaps because I made the mistake of testing my power over him:

I told him that I'd met two young students in class, one of whom had said, "So what d'you say, let's have some beer after class?" and the other had offered to carry my books, which immediately sparked a big fight between them.

And the music professor, he tried to pull them apart, and by accident, he got in-between them—in the line of fire, so to speak —which left him with a big bruise right there, under his eye. And sadly, he couldn't explain things as clearly as I'd hoped, on account of having to press a big icepack to his face.

Lenny tightened his lips, and when I saw his face my heart fell inside me.

I told him, real honest, that I'd ended up carrying my own books, and never had no beer with anyone but him, and that I didn't need no handsome boys when I already had him, that he was a grown-up, a smart, accomplished man, and that—no matter what happened—I would be his, only his, if only he would have me.

And while saying that, I opened my arms to him—but still, Lenny remained kinda distant, and he had an unfamiliar look on his face, which I couldn't figure out, like he didn't want nothing to do with me. The pleat in his forehead deepened and then, all of a sudden, he burst out with, "It is over, Anita."

Me, I didn't cry, didn't beg, didn't ask for no explanations, or hit him on the chest, even. Instead, I just froze there for a moment, with my arms still hanging, like, wide open in the air, and something went—boom!—exploding in my heart; after which I finally stirred, and went to the bedroom to collect my things, and looked for my hot pink high heels, which had rolled there, deep under the bed.

I stuffed them shoes into my backpack, along with my low-cut blouse and a pair of jeans and the course catalog, without wasting no time—not even once—to wipe my tears with my sleeve.

Lenny came right after me and leaned on the bedroom door, to stop me from bolting out. And he said, now in a changed voice, "Wait, Anita. It is not what you think."

So I slapped the backpack over my shoulders, and got up and rose to the tips of my toes to kiss him—long and hard—on his mouth, so he would have something to remember me by. And then I stormed past him, pushing my way out.

He rushed to the balcony, and from there, leaning over his desk, he cried after me, "Anita, stop! Just stop, will you? Let me explain..."

And running to the street I cried back, for the whole neighborhood to hear, 'cause I wasn't the one who had something to hide, "Forget it, Lenny! I don't want no explanation from you—not now, not ever!"

Which was the moment he said, and his voice sounded pretty painful, even from the distance, "She is back. That is why it is over. It just has to be over, now."

This marked the beginning of turmoil, of several years full of doubts and suspicions, with more ups-and-downs than the Ferris Wheel, down there on the Pier, and the Roller Coaster, combined. His wife, Natasha, came back, and she stayed for a while. Then she went away, finding a place to live here and there, perhaps with one of her girlfriends or with aunt Hadassa, or elsewhere.

And each time I moved back in with Lenny, she managed, somehow, to return. And me, I had to leave, 'cause like, I didn't want to have to face her. So I went back home to ma's place, swearing I won't want to see him no more. Finally, about five years ago, she left, this time for good, but like, who knows. And since then I haven't heard nothing about her—not from Lenny, not from anyone else.

Meanwhile, I've gone ahead with the Piano course, even though I've given up any hope on extending my stubby thumb, or growing my fingers any longer. And from time to time I would buy some piano sheet music for beginners, like *Caprice* by Paganini, and practice it—but only in school, and never when he's around, 'cause them keys, they may stick under my fingers, which would make my song stutter—and Lenny expects me to be perfect. He expects me to be her.

Which is why—in spite of me working so hard to try, to become better—he still complains.

Like, I've learned more ways to say things, and improved my vocabulary. I'm awful proud of saying *vocabulary*; which in plain talk means I have a lot of new words up here, in my head, which can confuse me sometimes, and even leave me speechless— unless I sound them out loudly, right away. Even so, Lenny says that my grammar is atrocious. I am, in his words, a *work in progress*. I wonder if she ever felt as choked by him—I mean, by what he expects—as I do.

And so I'm sitting here in the dark, in front of her piano, folded over my stomach because of this sharp pain, which makes me scared silly. I wish ma was here, 'cause like, even if she would give me a good slap, still, at least I could feel a touch, which would be better than this sorry state of being here, in the back of beyond.

Me, I'm so lonely I want to wail, to cry, to wash away the hurt—but my eyes, they're burning. They're dry, like, completely. I guess that being depressed is so much better when you can't shed a tear.

So instead I raise my head and with wild, vicious force, I bang my forehead, then bang it again against the keyboard. I'm free now, so free to attack it. The beast wakes up, and from its belly springs a sharp, fierce cry, which makes the air tremble in bursts, short bursts coming at me, doubled by echoes from every wall, every corner.

Meanwhile, in the background, I can hear them blinds, like, smacking each other, and giving way, suddenly, to a gust of wind. And there, in the opening of the glass door, which leads to the balcony, I spot his outline, standing behind the tape recorder.

The moonlight shines briefly on his shoulders as Lenny crosses the threshold. With a slight limp he makes his way in, and leans over my shoulders. And I can feel his strong arms wrapping around mine, arresting me, blocking my attempt to bang, bang, bang the keys. He turns me around—but me, I try to refuse him, and I fight like a savage, like a cat, and something surges in me, so in my fury I push him, I shove him away real hard, till he falls to his knees before me.

It's then that he locks his hands around me, and all of a sudden he lays his head, so tender like, in my lap. And there, in the dark, I touch his forehead, surprised to find not only the usual pleat—the one that brings back to me a memory of my pa —but a few more wrinkles, screwed up over his eyes. Which makes me figure out his expression: tormented.

So I hold myself back from saying, Where was you, I was awful lost here, all by myself for so many hours, and I thought that for sure, you've gone away. And instead I caress him, and take his face between my hands, and smooth his forehead with a kiss, asking, "What is it, what happened? Lenny, you crying?"

In place of an answer he fumbles in his shirt pocket, and from there gets his bifocals—even though the only thing to see here, in the darkness, is a patch of moonlight, which is blurry anyway, even with perfect vision; and the only thing to read is my face.

He puts the glasses on, like, to hide behind them; which makes me wonder. During the last ten years I've learned there's something about his wife, Natasha, something he conceals not only from me, but from his son, even. So I reckon it must be laying heavily on his mind.

"Oh, Lenny," I say, "just tell me what it is, will you? How hard can it be, to stop being the keeper of secrets?"

"I am worse than that," he says. "I am the inventor of lies."

"You're a writer," I shrug. "So, you make things up. What's so wrong with that?"

He turns away from me to wipe something in his eye, which makes me figure that he's shutting himself off.

So I try again. This time I say, "Let me read your stories."

"No," he says. "My writing is not the place where the fiction is."

"But Lenny," I plead, "don't you think you could make things so much easier, for you and me and everyone else, if only you said something real, like, if you told me the truth?"

He shakes his head, refusing me, trying to pull himself out of my hold, which makes me lose my balance and fall to my knees opposite him, right there on the floor, between the claws of the piano, so that now we're face to face.

There's more light now, which brings out more of him. And so, seeing him in such an agony I say, "You've taught me so much, Lenny. I note every one of your words, especially the ones I don't hardly get. I repeat them in my head, so that later I can figure out what they mean, and even use them, instead of just saying *things*."

"All I know," he blurts out, "is this: the words you learn—she forgets."

He don't really name her—but we both recognize who it is he's talking about. By now I know that Lenny knows that I don't want no explanations from him, no matter how hard he gets, or how closed his face becomes. I'm not one to pry—but then again, maybe the time's come for him to try, like, try to confide in me. Maybe prying things open isn't such a bad idea.

And so I suggest, "Why not tell me something about her?"

"No," he says, biting his lips. "I have said too much already."

Me, I watch him in silence, and before I can say nothing he adds, "No. There is no way for you to understand, to take in what she is going though."

"Maybe not," I say. "But just, try me."

"No," he repeats, a third time. "Yesterday, I tried to tell Ben, which was a mistake, a big mistake. Oh hell... What kind of a father am I? I should have kept my mouth shut, because since then he has left, and stayed out all night, who knows where. And with these legs under me, I can do no better than sit there, on the balcony with the tape recorder, and just, let my mind wander... *Rewind, Play, Rewind, Play*... I will never forgive myself if
—"

"*Stop*, just stop it! Stop torturing yourself," I cut in. "Maybe he just needs some time alone."

He turns his head away, over his shoulder, and glances at the thin, vertical intervals, right there between them blinds. By now you can start to detect, as if by reflection, a balcony. It's kinda identical to ours, and cast back from the other building, the building directly there, opposite us.

It seems like Lenny's trying to guess—by the graying of the dark—how much time until daybreak. He presses the sides of his head, till a vein flares up on his temple, pulsing there between the nails of his fingers.

"If anything happens to Ben it would be on me. It would be entirely my fault. My God," he says. "I should have buried the whole thing, and kept it there, in the grave."

He don't speak no more after that.

By now, the night is almost gone. It's peeling away, like an old, silvery blue wallpaper, rolling in from the corners. There, in the balcony facing us, an old woman comes out in a loosely tied bathrobe, rubbing her eyes, kinda sleepy. She waters her plants, floods her dry geranium, then goes back inside, pulling the sliding glass door shut behind her, with a long, deafening screech.

Lenny winces. I can tell: this isn't what he's listening for.

Now, more familiar sounds: a car is being started in the parking area, making a knocking noise, 'cause it's an old clunker and the engine is still cold. Finally it lurches, somehow, into the street and you can hear it like, turning away, even as the brakes of another car is being stepped on, followed by a sudden, rubbery squeal.

This isn't what he's listening for.

It's Morning. You can hear water gushing through the pipes inside the walls, because there, in the apartment next door, someone has just started taking a shower. Meanwhile, in the garden below, the sprinklers come on, spluttering water one spit after another.

This isn't what he's listening for.

For him, all them sounds are being drowned out by the tick, the incessant tick, tick, tick of the old alarm clock. The little hammer on top of it is idle, and so is the twin bells. They're just hanging there, left and right of the hammer, reflecting this whole room, and the piano, and us, too. We seem so unlike ourselves, bent out of shape in their brass finish.

So tense, so distorted, so small.

It's almost six. The hour hand's dropped down, as if defeated, at last, by the force of gravity, a force which the minute hand is still trying to fight. Now it seems to have come to a stop. It's stuck there, just short of its mark.

I stare at it thinking, I should get up from the floor already. I should take hold of the clock, ignoring its curvy surface, which shows a mirror image of my hand, and of my split lifeline. I should wind up the key, right there in the back of it, so that time's gonna move forward, and the little hammer at the top's gonna hurry up and at last, strike them bells.

Just then, quick footsteps can be heard, climbing the stairs. And by the rhythm I know who it is—and so does Lenny.

So we hold each other and struggle, somehow, to our feet, and I hand him his crutch so he can reach the entrance door, in a big hurry, and like, greet his son.

And watching him as he turns away from me, I think to myself, He's afraid, he don't want to tell me nothing—but still, I'm glad he's started to open the door for Ben.

Things could be so much simpler. If only...

How sad it is that at this moment, when Lenny is injured and here, behind him, I'm holding my belly because of this dull pain, this is the time we keep ourselves apart, in an effort, a lame effort to play our game, play it now in front of the boy, as if, I swear, as if all is well.

Oh, at last—the alarm! The ringing of them bells! The sound of laughter... How lonely it must be, to be the keeper of secrets, the inventor of lies.

In My Defense

Chapter 5

In my defense I have this to say: When men notice me, when the lusty glint appears in their eyes, which betrays how, in their heads, they're stripping me naked—it's me they accuse of being indecent.

Problem is, men notice me all the time.

How can a girl like me ever claim to be innocent? Even if I haven't done nothing wrong, I'm already soiled, simply because of their dirty thoughts.

And sometimes, it's because of their actions. Like the time I was twelve, and Johnny shoved me into the bathroom and pinned me to the floor. And afterwards, he pointed his finger at me, saying *I made him do it,* 'cause to him, I looked sexy, more sexy even than my ma, whom he was gonna take on a date, just as soon as she would come back from her evening shift and like, freshen up. But I, he said, was fresh anyhow.

So I try to forget the yellow stain at the foot of the toilet, and the hard, sticky floor, both of which took care of the freshness all right—but still, to this day I go on learning how to live with the blame.

And it don't matter, really, if I try to keep my eyes lowered, and stay out of the way, and wrap myself in something modest, like this old, rumpled blanket which I've just fetched from the sofa, 'cause any second now, they may be coming in here.

So I bundle myself, bringing the corners of the blanket under my arms, and tying them tightly over my breast, so the edge winds up gathering the flesh, a bit like the pleats of a curtain. Oh shoot, I don't hardly care! I've come to dislike the way I look, and dread that thing in me, which they see as a *power*—but I know as a curse.

The more bewitched they claim to be by the way I look—the more I reckon I'm in danger. I swear, I've had it up to here with men who say they was ruined by a woman.

In the end, they tend to recover, and one way or another build themselves back up. And they do it, without fail, by destroying her. So, like ma says: to keep myself out of trouble, and my name clean, it's *strength* that I need—not power.

Which is why I've turned away, the moment Ben came in and was kissed by his pa. I knew right away that I must put as much distance as I can between us. Even there, from across the room, I could feel, like, something which couldn't be denied, passing between his eyes and mine, behind Lenny's back.

Right now, Ben's trying to shrink away. His back's kinda bent, his shoulders—angled forward, like, to defend himself, in his own timid way, from his father, and from any further contact, any further show of love. And his gaze, hanging heavy under those long, dark lashes, seems so sad, so full of regret, because of a moment, a brief moment of joy being held in that embrace.

The features of his face, they're so fine. They seem to be penciled in. By some mother-like instinct—which is totally new to me—I can tell Ben's kinda lost. He's like a boy, longing to feel the worn-out, familiar feel of his mama's apron, and breathe her good smell, and just stand there, giving himself up, and crying, and waiting for her to wipe his wet face, and take away the hurt.

In my head I can only imagine how shocked he must feel—despite knowing about Lenny and me—to find me in this place, instead of his ma. You can tell he's swamped, totally swamped by this new reality, as well as by his memories, and like, hopelessly sunk in his daydreams. Somewhere deep inside, he wants me to be her.

I bet he has an old, vague image of his ma, from a long time ago. By the way he looks at me, I reckon he can find her, somehow, in my face. For him, I ain't here at all. I'm see-through.

When Ben realizes his mistake, he seems to become annoyed. I bet he's worried, worried about his ma, and about the past that keeps haunting him, keeps coming up to the surface. Me, I can't even define how he relates to me, exactly, 'cause it keeps changing. In the last two days, ever since I met Ben, I've found him confused—and confusing:

I pity him, seeing how consumed he is by desire. His entire body is like, burning up. And his eyes, they're fluttering around me until—like a moth heading, in a roundabout way, into a light source—they connect with mine. I can sense his hate sometimes, and at once pull back from him, 'cause I spot how hard his jaw is set, and even, how murderous the spark right there, in that shadow under his lashes, which reminds me of some animal, getting pretty tense, like, getting ready for the kill.

And so, while Lenny and his son huddle together by the door, exchanging words, I sneak out of the living room. First, I tighten the blanket again across my chest. Then I rush past them, across the hall and the corridor, and into the bedroom. From the closet

I pull out an ice-blue, long sleeve dress. It's hers—but all the same, I put it on. It fits. I'm safe. I'm shielded.

After a while I notice that their voices, which have been flaring out in heated talk, have given way to silence. So I crack my door open, and listen, and I can't hear nothing at all, so I tiptoe down the corridor.

And from here I catch sight of Lenny, lying there across the sofa. After a night with no sleep, fatigue must have caught up to him. His glasses, they're askew: one lens magnifies the high forehead, the other—his thinning, sleeked-back hair.

My heart aches, it goes out to him: his lips, they're tight even now, guarding the gate, like, the gate between being awake and dreaming. He don't talk in his sleep, not even a word—but right now a snore escapes, quite by surprise, from the corner of his mouth. His arms, they're folded across his chest, like he's holding himself prisoner.

And around the corner, there's a sound of steps, so I know Ben's there. He's pacing back and forth, this way and that around the walls, like, to measure his cage, same as his father.

I turn back and the minute I mount the bed, I hear someone rapping softly on the closed door, saying, "Anita?"

"What is it, Ben," I ask, bluntly. "What d'you want?"

His voice is muffled. "Nothing," he says. "I—I hope you are feeling better this morning," he says. "I think I am going out, in just a few minutes, to see my mother. I mean, to visit—"

Which takes me completely by surprise, 'cause since she disappeared, I've been waiting to hear word about Natasha. From time to time I would ask Lenny—only to get a kiss and nothing, nothing else in return. So, for the last five years I

49

reckoned she don't want him to speak. I reckoned it's for her sake he's silent.

So now I fling the door open, and as I face Ben I let slip, "You gonna visit her? Like, where? I mean, she's back?"

"He did not tell you anything about her, did he," he says, stating rather than asking. I don't even have to say it, Ben knows. I can tell he's been through secrets. Like me, he's been fooled. He totally gets how it feels.

And so I have to lie, "Tonight, for sure, Lenny's gonna reveal everything. Really, I swear."

Ben tries to say something, which curls his lips in a strange way. If not for the bitter look, you could call it laughter. "Would you like to know? Would you? Would you want me to tell you," he advances, "right here, right now?"

"No," I insist, hoping he can't see through me. "I'd rather *he* did."

"I see," he shrugs.

And so I counter, "Do you," and then we're just waiting there, on each side of the threshold, not knowing what to say and where to go from here.

Finally Ben comes up with, "So here, here is something I wanted to ask you. Forgive me, I know nothing, really, about you —but please, try to put yourself in my place. Suppose you were going to visit your mother, and wanted to remind her, I mean, about the past. About your childhood, perhaps—"

"The past? My ma isn't too fond of that. I won't bring it up with her, if I was you—but of course, if you was to pay her, that's totally different: she used to be a fortune teller, for real. I bet she could tell you a thing or two about the future."

With a confused look, he passes a hand through his tousled hair, trying to smooth it the same way as his father—only in his case, it resists and falls right back, over his brow. "Please," says Ben. "Help me... There is no one else. I mean, no one I can trust. And it is not easy for me to try, to beg you for an answer. I find it nearly impossible, to seek advice like this, without giving up something, some information about my mother; which apparently, you do not even want to hear."

"So," I say, "just don't," which makes him angry.

"You," he snaps, "you must find all of this strange, and much too ambiguous."

"Ambigu-what?" I say. "Just tell me plainly, Ben: what is it you want?"

He stands there, kneading his hands, looking kinda torn. "Mom and I, we have not talked for a long while," he admits. "I want her to be able to look back, somehow... I mean, I want her not to forget. Now, how would you go about it?"

In spite of the pity I feel for him, I don't really want to help him. It's gonna go against me, 'cause Natasha is my enemy even when she isn't here. If she wanted to, I reckon she could take my power away.

Go, go away already, I tell him in my mind—but aloud I say, "Just talk to her. She's gonna get it."

"No, I am afraid she won't," he says, grimly.

Against my interest I pity him again, this time for being so full of doubts, and so sad, and most of all, isolated.

"Just tell her a story," I suggest. "Bring up something, anything from the heart."

"I cannot. I do not know how," he mumbles, painfully.

Me, I must be out of my mind to try to take him out of a tight spot; which in spite of myself, I'm getting closer to doing. "Think of something you share, both of you. You're gonna be surprised, she's gonna listen. She's gonna tell you stories about you, which you don't even know about yourself."

"No," he says, with a grave tone in his voice. "I doubt she can."

And I say, "Wait—wait here, don't move. I have an idea."

Which is the moment when, because of that stupid sense of pity, I ignore this feeling, down in my guts, that tells me to shut the door in his face. Instead, I make a bad mistake: leaving the it open I take a step back, and roll myself over the bed, all the way across, to Lenny's side. And from his drawer I pull out an album, a thick album with a metal clasp, which locks over the gilded edge of its pages, about which I know: I'm not supposed to know nothing.

Still, I can tell you that there's one picture, one special picture missing there, in the middle of the second page.

The reason I'm so sure about it, if you must know, is that it took me a few tries—first by trying to pick the corner, then by heating the glue with my hairdryer, which kinda damaged the surface, and later, by threading a floss under it—to remove the picture and finally, stash it away.

"Here," I say coming back, carrying the album to him. "You must know this album, right? Just look at it together, you and your ma. The rest's gonna come easy, I promise."

He smiles, like he's overcome by a thrill. As if being greeted by an old friend, he passes a hand, so tender like, over the cover, feeling the fine cracks in the leather, the raised spine.

Meanwhile, he lets me go on holding the thing. So by now I have to support it with both hands, it's awful heavy. At last I give up. I take a step back and sit there, on the edge of the bed. Ben draws closer. He unlocks the clasp. Now he's spreading the pages wide open, right here in my lap, over my wrists.

And together we look at the pages: how they're turning yellow along the edges, how brown spots are like, blossoming all over them, and how them photos look faded, even though they're protected, under the seal of clear plastic sheets. On each page there's glue, lined in strips. It holds the photos in place— but also, because of the acid in it, destroys them.

"God," he lets out. "It takes so much guessing to study these images. Just like a memory: you are left clinging to something which now, is no longer a record. Instead, it is just... Nothing. I mean, nothing more than a hint, a suggestion."

With a clap Ben shuts the album, and takes it off my hands, and slips it under his jacket. So now it's held in place by the close-fitting waistband, and pressed to his chest by both arms. Already I see him standing kinda taller, more erect than earlier this morning. I bet it's because of the weight, the extra weight he's carrying now, next to his heart.

Like ma says: the heavier the load—the more you straighten yourself. For me this is something new, something that only now that I'm pregnant, I begin to understand.

My hands, they're empty now, and like, I can't give him no help no more. Which wakes me up to a change: from the corner of his eye, he's looking down at me, and a glint flashes there, under his lashes, a glint which I've come to know all too well. It exposes his desire, his craving to touch me. To him, who cares what I have to lose. Like, who cares that I'm carrying a baby inside. Who cares whose wife I am, or whose son he is. Who cares how we got to this place.

Suddenly here we are: a man and a woman and nothing in between—other than a tremble in the air, and a thrill, the sharp thrill of danger.

In a blink of an eye I can see the trap, and I hate him for setting it up—even if he did so without intent. And I hate, hate, hate myself for being caught in it. Sooner or later, my innocence is gonna be called into question, and who's gonna believe a girl like me?

This brings back a memory of ma calling me *Bitch*, because of what happened back then, when I was twelve, between Johnny and me. Me, I argued with her, insisting that no, don't call me that, I get to decide who I am and what I am, and what I would be, I—and nobody else but me. And she countered that if he'd touched me, we already knew—beyond any doubt—what I'd become.

At this point the only thing, the only barrier that seems to make Ben stumble, and holds him back from taking me, is the sight of the dress—which Natasha used to wear—hanging stiffly, kinda like ice, over my body. I find myself grateful, awful grateful to her, 'cause in a way, she's shielding me.

This way, he can't strip me naked—not even in his mind.

So I gather my strength, and before he can pour out his feelings, and confess to have fallen, like, under my power, and tell me he's ruined, all because of me, I wave my hand and tell him to go, go away already.

Ben seems unhappy to be dismissed so casually. I bet he's thinking me cruel to him. He's asking himself, like, Why is the bitch playing so hard to get? She's drawn me here, to her bed—hasn't she? He seems so unsure about himself, about what, if anything, he is supposed to do now. But if he's feeling ashamed, it's not for wanting his old man's woman—but sadly, for what he considers his own flow, his show of impotence.

He hesitates, then turns slowly, to walk out of the bedroom; at which time I can swear I see an outline there, over his shoulder, far in the depth of the corridor. Maybe I'm seeing things, but—for just a second—I detect a flash, reflected like, in someone's glasses.

Down there in the shadow, someone's recording every detail, listening to every damn whisper of this scene.

Record. Play: a man and a woman, and nothing in between.

I want to ask, Is it you? Is it you, Lenny? Why ain't you coming to my help? But instead, I just slam the door shut. All I want to be is alone. Why do I feel guilty when I haven't done nothing wrong.

Then I raise the corner of the mattress, which is where I've stashed away that old picture, the one that was glued in the middle of the second page of the album. The sight of it calms me down, at first.

I pick it up and study every detail—like I've done so many times before—because like, the image may go on fading, until in the end, nothing's gonna be left. I'm so charmed by it. This moment delights me as if I had lived it, even though—or maybe because—it's stolen.

In it, a baby is about to be lifted from a cradle by his mama. His face, it's awful close to the surface—but barely visible. You can only guess it, 'cause the paper is a bit damaged, and most of the lines is like, out of focus—except for a dark contour, which is still intact, marking the shadow of his long, curved lashes.

I put a hand to my belly, and touch my lips to the image, right there, over that shadow. I wonder if this is how my baby's gonna look, and marvel at the thought of how his eyes would change when he wakes, or falls asleep, or rolls them, like, in the sphere of his dreams, and then later, when he grows up to become a man, 'cause it's so easy to fill in the details on a page that's like, almost blank.

On the other side, right there behind the cradle, the mother —whose lips, and cheeks, and freckled nose, they're all just like mine—she's leaning over him, with open arms.

Her face is serious, without the slightest smile. She's looking directly at the camera, at the one taking the picture, whom I've previously imagined to be Lenny—but today, I find a change in her. This time, it's me she is facing.

The way she looks at me is severe, critical, even disapproving. I bet it's because the laugh lines have dimmed with time. But then, her eyes! Oh God, they're so clear, so full of pure, glorious light; which, for a moment, brings me close to despair. I'm in awe. Look, I have goosebumps! The two of us look the same, just like sisters—but oh, how I wish I could be more like her!

Me, I don't have nothing more I want to say in my defense— except to ask you again: put yourself in my place. How can a girl like me ever claim to be innocent?

The Family We Are

Chapter 6

The moment I come out of the bedroom—trying to forget what's just happened between Ben and me—that's the moment I see Lenny standing there, next to the entrance door. He takes a step forward to reach me, which alerts me at once to a threat, 'cause I've seen him jealous before.

Me, I can tell how he must be feeling right now, 'cause I've been there myself. From time to time, I would drive myself crazy thinking about him and Natasha, about her coming back here, or him going away with her. Then like, I would fly at him, with fire in my heart, crying that I hate, hate, hate him, and that I couldn't take his secrets no more, and whatever! And no matter what Lenny would say, I would end up going into a jealous rage.

Rage, it can like, scorch everything around you, and make it all rise up in smoke, till you don't hardly know who's your friend and who—your enemy, so you can't really trust no one. And most of all, you can't trust the one you hold dear.

At such moments I find that I miss being with my ma, who threw me out of her place long ago. I miss her, because inside— where no one else can see—I'm still a child, and because with her I'm at ease, and I don't have to torture myself, and I don't have doubts about nothing, 'cause she makes things cut and dried, even if she has to slap me for it.

So even though we're married now, I don't really feel I belong here, in this place. An outcast: that's me.

So I storm past him—but Lenny lays his hand on me. Grabbing me by the shoulder, he brings me to a standstill.

"*Stop*! Stop, Anita," he says. "We have to talk."

"Whatever," I say, "I'm done talking," even though we both reckon that like, the only thing I've swapped with him since this morning was my silence for his.

And he goes, "Maybe *you* are—but I am not."

And I don't say nothing, 'cause like, what's the point? Between his son and me, I bet I know whose story he's gonna believe.

And so he presses on, "There is something, Anita, something I must tell you."

"What," I say. "You leaving me again, Lenny?"

"Going back to work," he says, which takes the wind right out of me.

"Really?" I gape at him, and notice that his briefcase is right there on the floor, at his feet. "So soon? You sure you're up to it? Like, with the limping and all?"

"Yes," he says, and lets go of me. "It is time. I cannot afford staying home any longer."

And, seeing that I stare at him as if to ask, Now, what does that mean, he goes on to say, "It means, jobs are hard to come by, Anita. Especially," he adds, "at my age."

"Fine, then," I say, and lift his briefcase from the floor, to save him the trouble, and I hand the thing to him. But instead of taking it, he grips me again, this time by my waist, and turns me to the light, like, to read me.

"It is not Ben I want to talk to you about," he says.

I wonder if he can tell what's in the back of my mind, which is the place I keep words, words too long to make any sense, and other things I'm trying to forget.

"Really?" I say, hearing sudden relief in my voice. "It isn't?"

And I press my head to his chin till I feel him wiggling his upper lip, 'cause my hair is frizzy, and so it must be tickling his nose. And through the fabric, the thin cotton of this dress, I feel his hands on my body, his flesh against mine, and it's coming forward, so I reckon he wants me, like, awful hard.

"Take it off," says Lenny.

So I slip the dress off, 'cause it don't belong to me, but to Natasha. Wearing it must have been a mistake, 'cause this thing brings her back to him, and for some reason, it brings out other feelings, which I'm not sure I get, exactly. So I step out of it, and see it puddling there, on the floor, like a piece of blue ice, melting.

Then, on the whim of a moment, I rise to the tips of my toes and stretch for a kiss; which he denies me. And instead, Lenny looks straight into my eyes, saying, "In a word: I want you to know that maybe, I have lied to you."

Now, that's just like him: lying to me; which he then doubts; which he wants me to know, so he's protected from guilt.

And before I can point it out, or ask him why anyone would say, *In a word*, only to follow it with a full sentence—and a long one at that—Lenny goes on to say, "I have told you, just a minute ago, that I do not wish to talk about my son. But now that I think about it, maybe I have lied."

I can see my image flashing across one lens, then the other, right there in his glasses. And it looks kinda small, and odd, too, 'cause each one of them surfaces is like, a bit curved. There... Now my image has met the frame. It's gone, vanished into thin air.

Me, I'm feeling, like, a tinge of shame—even though I didn't do nothing wrong. So I'm waiting on edge, right there in front of him, now with my eyes lowered, holding my breath to hear him, 'cause who knows what he thinks he's seen.

To me, he's the witness, and he's the judge, a judge with a bias in favor of the other side. And here's the accused, ready for the verdict. Here I am.

Lenny starts talking to me, and what he says isn't nothing like what I've expected, and it takes my breath away.

"You may be looking at my son," he says, "and at me. You may be watching us, thinking, These are strange people. This is not a family I would want to live next door to, let alone in the same home—but this, Anita, is the family we *are*."

And in a whisper I repeat, "Yes, we are."

And something makes me warm all over at the mere sound of what he's just said, 'cause like, if even he, Lenny, don't barely know what's strange and what's not, then who knows? Is there anyone normal, out there? What is it exactly, *normal?*

And I don't mind me being odd, when so are they, when so are all of us.

And I can see how, in the days to come, I'm gonna have to find my way, somehow, between them two men, 'cause I get it: Lenny needs his son, and he can't risk another split, another tear between the two of them. We must all try, as best we can, to forgive each other, and to accept us, accept the way we are.

I find myself awful glad to be near him, 'cause at this moment I ain't an outcast no more: he's made me a part of something which—even if it's damaged—still, all the same, it's as close as you can get to being whole.

"We," I echo, "are a family."

"A family," he admits, "with a load of secrets."

Lenny raises his eyes to the ceiling as if to find the right words, which must be kinda hard for him, 'cause now he takes his briefcase from me and like, tries to take cover behind it. At last he lets out a sigh.

"What I have to say," he tells me, "is about her."

In return to which I let slip, "It always is."

He backs away, so I tell him, "Lenny—don't you stop! I'm here, listening."

And he says, "You may remember that time, five years ago, when Natasha came back, and you left, swearing it was all over between us."

And me, I nod, "I do."

And Lenny says, "I tried very hard to mend things with her. If we could start over, if life could go back to the way things used to play out, it would have meant so much! Not only for us —but for Ben, too."

"Natasha," he says, "had stopped giving piano lessons by then, and from time to time she would seem—how shall I describe it?—withdrawn. In spite of this, she acted as if all was fine, and so did I. For the most part, we were getting closer again, so who could ask for more? She and I managed, somehow, to settle into a daily routine—until one evening, just before going to bed, the phone rang. I picked it up on my side of the bed; she—on hers."

His lips tighten, and for a long while he don't say much; which forces me to ask, "So, who was it?"

And he says, "It was her doctor."

And me, I ask, "What, was she sick?"

And Lenny says, "Yes," which seems to take a lot out of him, 'cause now he's turning pale. "She was," he reveals. "And still is."

And so I run to the kitchen and bring him a chair and have him sit there and try, and catch his breath. Then I bring him a glass of water, which at first he tries to refuse.

So I give him a look. "In a word," I tell him, "drink!"

So, he drinks; after which I ask, with caution, "So—what did the doctor tell you?"

He's raising his eyes again, but the right words can't be found nowhere close to him—not on the ceiling, or on the wall, or the floor, in this corner, or that. So instead, Lenny shuts his eyes and, like, stumbles into saying, "The doctor, he said: Mr. Kaminsky, the tests came back."

"At this point," he recalls, "I took a hard swallow. The doctor paused briefly—perhaps taking another look at the test results—and then went on to say, I have some difficult news for you. Your wife, I believe, has a form of Alzheimer's."

I take the briefcase away from him, 'cause it's just about to fall, anyway.

And so Lenny can't brace himself no more, 'cause at this point, he don't have nothing to hold on to, and nowhere to hide. Instead he just sits there, with the empty glass, saying, "Alzheimer's," and then again, in a voice that is nearly gagged, "Alzheimer's."

And after a long pause he adds, "At the sound of this word, Natasha was confused and I—I dropped to my knees. I remember, she could not get it, could not understand what was going on and told the doctor, Wait, hold on, I cannot talk to you now. Call back later, something is wrong here. No, not with me —with my husband."

Lenny takes off his glasses and like, wipes something from the corner of his eye, and my heart goes out to him. And then, then the strangest thing starts happening to me. For the first time in ten years I feel not only for him—but for her, too.

I pity her, which surprises me, and allows me to watch the whole scene in my head, as if—by some magic—a curtain's risen, and I find myself right there to watch, or like, to snap a picture of the past, of that moment between them:

I see him crouched there, on the floor at the foot of the bed; and her plopping the phone in its cradle, to stop it already, stop that voice, that muffled voice that keeps coming back, saying, Hello? Hello? Is anyone there?

I hear her coming over, wrapping her arms around his, and asking, like, What's wrong, what's wrong, Lenny; and him saying, No, dear, it's nothing, I promise, nothing at all, really, and sobbing, sobbing with no tears and no sound.

I bet he knows that from that moment on, he would be alone, really alone, and that he must go on, and keep this thing under wraps, so that no one who's known her before would ever think to put her name and that word—that horrific word—in the same sentence, or anywhere close to each other.

And before I can snap another picture of her, and place it there, in the back of my mind, I see her walking away. Her robe's like, flapping behind her, letting the light shine through, and then—poof!—she's gone, perhaps to turn off the bedside lamp. Still, I can't get rid of the ghost of her image. It still kinda hangs there, like the end of a shadow, a long shadow left there, in the center of a picture, even after the body itself has crossed out of the frame, and has long vanished.

This, now, is the way I draw her in my head: coming back, like, to touch him softly, to ask what's the matter, what has happened here. At times she's like, clinging, at times hovering there, over his shoulders, a faint trace of a thing, turning fainter with time; one that can't remind him no more of her, her whom he knew: The mother, the wife she was. The girl she used to be.

So I take a step closer to Lenny, and this time I don't allow myself to be stopped—not by him, not by that shadow, and not by nothing else I've seen in my head, just now. And I brush my lips over his hair, and spread my arms real wide, hugging her hugging him.

I can't see his face, 'cause it's hanging down, like it's buried between his shoulders. "I must be going," he mumbles from deep down. "I must be going. I cannot be late for work."

And standing here, by his side, I let him lean on me, so he can rise, somehow, to his feet. Lenny turns his back on me and a minute later, the sound of his footfalls can be heard, one thump after another, shaking the stairs.

And after a while, it kinda blends away into the other noises, till you can't tell it from the hum of traffic down there, in the street.

Now I close the door. At long last, this I know: I don't need an answer no more for that question, the one that confused me so, the one I've been asking myself, with such pain, such agony, for the last ten years. And I won't need to guess, not anymore, why he told me—that first time, when we danced—that I, I reminded him of a girl he used to know.

Go Back To Your Mama

Chapter 7

Lenny's gone, but still, I'm thinking about him, about how he's touched on that time, the lost time nearly five years ago, when I went out the door, swearing I ain't gonna come back to him, not ever. What he hasn't said—and what left such a bitter taste in my mouth—is how he told me, back then, "You are a nice kid, Anita. Go, go back to where you came from. Go back to your mama."

And what he don't know is that ma wasn't all too happy to see me, "Because," she said, "I told you so, didn't I? Didn't I say, he's gonna grow tired of you, and dump you before you know it? He's gonna go back to his wife, 'cause it's her that he wants— not you! And if not her, then—then, it must be something else with him, always something else, like, looking for other women. Maybe they remind him, somehow, of that thing, who knows what it is, which he found in her. Maybe what he's really looking for is just, like, the *idea* of her."

And when I mumbled, "Whatever," ma said, "I knew it! She can twist him around her little finger, if she wants to."

She didn't tell me nothing else about this thing, this *idea of her*, which ma thought was fixed, somehow, in Lenny's head, like some piece of music; and I, I didn't ask. Instead, I bought a six-pack for her and a six-pack for me, and we sat down on her pillows, on the narrow iron bed, drinking beer; she talking, me weeping all night, after which ma wiped my face, and grabbed the palm of my hand—like she used to do in the old days—to read it.

And she told me to stay put, to wait for her, 'cause she had something crucial, something real big to tell me, like, about the future. I reckon she saw *some* clue of what was coming—but didn't quite grasp it, not in full, anyway, 'cause the next thing you know, ma went out, came back a second later, picked the empty beer bottles, and took them with her. Along the way she gave me a peck, smack in the middle of my forehead, which surprised me.

Then, having kissed me goodbye, she went out again, and then... Then, on her way to work, right there on the corner of Euclid Street—Bang! I could hear the sound, out there—she was killed in a car accident.

I stayed in her place till the end of the month—but couldn't stay longer, 'cause me, I didn't have no money to pay for the rent, on account of not having a job. So I started moving from one place to another, trying to hide behind someone's garage, or in a little cove on the beach. Sometimes I shared a room with this friend, or the other. After a while, I lost count of all the places where I'd lived. Which is why I don't want to ever think about finding a new place again.

A few months later—I can't even say how many—I was walking, like, in a daze down the street, and raised my eyes from the ground. I found myself on the Pier, staring at the swirly, painted letters of the ice cream place. And then, in a flash, it hit me: this, this was the place, the very same place where we had met, Lenny and me, that first time.

I backed away, all shook up. Words started drifting in my head. I thought about him, and about how far away, even absurd the whole thing was, I mean, like, the idea of us together.

And I thought about the hunger, and them buckets inside, full of chopped nuts and cherries and coconut flakes. The air trembled, and in it I caught a sniff of cream, and a whiff of waffle cones, which at once awakened the pain, right here in my stomach. How strange it was to be back here again—only this time, on the outside, 'cause that's, like, a totally different place—even if most people don't really care to know it.

My feet carried me, somehow, till I stopped right there, under the *Santa Monica* signboard, which arched over the entrance to the pier. And no way, I swear, there's no way you could even begin to guess my surprise when all of a sudden, I spotted Lenny up there, behind the large window of *The Lobster*. Sitting inside, there he was, holding a margarita glass, laughing his head off, and like, having a real good time.

I could see the slice of lime on the lip of his glass, and closed my eyes—but still, was blocked from smelling it.

I tried, in vain, to bring back the touch of salt around the rim, and the scent of butter on mashed potatoes, and the meaty flavor of wild mushrooms, and the pleasure you get with every gulp of hot, thick clam chowder. I could almost lick the spoon, and pinch the bread, and wipe the bowl with it, 'cause I had known all that. Me, I had been there with him, like, a lifetime ago.

I leaned over the railing of the pier, and for a second hoped he would see me. How could he not, with my hair flaming red, and blowing, long and wild, in the winter wind, which swept across the divide?

Now I could see the girl sitting there, opposite him. She raised her glass and clinked it against his, then cuddled up to him, like, to whisper something up close, in his ear.

I don't hardly know if there was something odd with the air, which stirred past me with cloud after cloud of salty mist; or the sheet of glass over there, which must have had some flaws all over it; or the mirror image of sunset, which buckled out of shape, in and out of the flaws; or else, was it the film of tears, which formed in my eyes; or the sorrow, which came in like a tide, to wash over me—but in a blink, everything blurred.

Everything started swimming in front of me: like, the shadow of her little black dress, the flash of her gold earring, even the blond streaks in her hair. All of them things, which lived on the other side of the layers—the layer of mist, and of glass, and flaws, tears, wash—they all rippled a bit and then, settled into a haze.

I blinked again and at once, things went back to the way things should be—except that the girl was still there, by his side, where I should have been, had I not left him.

I had never met his wife before, but of one thing I was sure: this girl wasn't her.

She was no Natasha. I don't know how I could tell. Maybe it was the way she laughed, flinging her hair back, and batting her painted lashes, and opening her mouth real wide—but this I knew: this girl, she didn't have no class—but then, unlike me, she was bending over backwards, just to fake it.

When they came out of the restaurant, I couldn't help but follow them from a distance, like a stray kitten, holding back a purr, ready to roll over for the rub of a hand.

He hailed a cab and leaned into it, talking to the driver. For a minute I thought I caught Lenny glancing at me, over his shoulder, but no—maybe I only wished it. Then she kissed him. He opened the door for her. She climbed in, closed the door. He kinda waved, once. The cab merged into traffic, and away it went.

Meanwhile, I lost him in the crowd. A minute later I spotted him again. He was turning on his heels and oh, shoot! I couldn't believe it: he started weaving his way between this shoulder and that, walking back closer and closer, directly here, to me.

And my heart pounded—oh God! How it pounded!—so, so hard inside me; after which I hung down my head, hoping he didn't see me—or else, if he did, I was hoping that out of pity, he would turn away, 'cause I was too thin and too dirty, and didn't have nothing pretty to wear, all of which made people around me look away, or look right through me, like I wasn't there, even.

Me, I made a quick move, trying to slip away—but already, it was too late.

"My God," said Lenny, now facing me. "You look horrible."

What he said next blew me away. I felt like, this moment wasn't real, because in a softer voice he told me, "How I missed you."

For a second I wanted to say, Really? It don't look at all like you missed me, isn't it so, Lenny? And don't even think you can use me, and then like, walk all over me. I may look like shit right now. I reckon I do—but no, you ain't gonna dump me, never, never again! And anyway, where is she, where is the dear wife, Natasha?

But instead, in a meek tone, I said, "How can you even say you missed me. You, you told me to go away."

At that moment Lenny was lost for words, because he knew me, knew me well enough to get what I hadn't said, too. So he took off his winter coat and hung it around my shoulders, very gently, like he was afraid I would break, somehow. And suddenly, it felt kinda good.

"You are shivering," he said then.

"Me," I denied, "shivering?"

And he offered, "Let me take you home."

So I hid my face behind the collar of his coat, knowing it's gonna smell awful bad by the time I'm gonna have to give it back. "Home?" I said, and now my voice was muffled. "Me, I don't have a home."

"I meant," he corrected, "let us go home, together."

Which brought up the anger in me. "You," I raged, "I don't need you! And don't you think that I do—'cause I swear, I don't! You told me to go back, back where I came from. So here I am, Lenny. I'm down in the muck, deeper than deep."

He stretched out his hands to me, like he wanted to pull me in, to save me. And in spite of myself I flung the coat off, and shoved it, right there, into his open arms. "Take the stupid thing, and your pity, too! Stop acting so grand, and feeling so, so sorry for me! And you," I pointed, "*you* go back! Go the hell back where you came from!"

People started looking at me now. They whispered to one another and pointed at me, like I was naked or something, which made me hot, crazed even. I blushed. It felt kinda strange, being visible again. The anger surged in me, it threatened to burst out, like, any moment now. And Lenny tried to say something—but me, I won't let him.

I raged on, "Don't you dare say nothing to me now!"

And he said, like he didn't even hear me, "How I missed your voice."

And I said, "So listen to me, and listen good: I can get food, and I can get a place to sleep, and on a good day I can get a job, even! One day, Lenny, one day I'm gonna get back on my feet, I swear I will—and for sure, I'm gonna do it without you."

And he said, "I know it. I have no doubt about it." And then he added, "But Anita, I need you—"

"For that," I countered, "you can get that girl. I bet she's gonna come back to you, like, in the flick of a finger, and be fucking nice, Lenny, and spend the night."

"No," he said. "Now, you listen: it is *you* I need. I miss you."

"Don't," I said.

To which he said nothing, but his eyes did his pleading for him.

And I said, "You can't beg a beggar."

And he said, "You may not believe it. I do not believe it myself, when I hear myself saying it—but really, I even miss the way you speak."

And I said, "I ain't gonna talk fancy no more, Lenny."

And he said, "Not to worry: you never did."

So I had to make it extra clear to him, "I ain't gonna *enunciate* them words, like you told me to, Lenny."

"I understand," he said. "This is so incredible. I can listen to you all night long."

And I said, "You can?"

He took a step closer. "I should learn it from you, Anita."

"Learn what?"

And he wrapped his coat around me, even gentler than before. "Like, your way to say it."

"Say what?"

"Them words," he said, winking.

"You making fun of me?"

"No," he said, serious now. "It is so cold. Let us go now, Anita. Let us go home already."

In the five years since then, I've noticed a change in him. There wasn't that feeling no more, like he was waiting for something to happen, or for his wife to knock on the door, any moment now. Somehow, she wasn't there, which made me grow edgy. I couldn't fight her, 'cause how d'you fight air? How d'you crush it? How d'you know when to duck, or even, when you're open to attack?

In my mind, she's become a threat, an unseen presence, about which he refused to say a word.

And the heat between us has cooled off. I would dab some perfume on my wrist, and light a candle next to the bed—but instead of coming in, Lenny would stay out there, on the balcony, perhaps to write, or to press them keys on his tape recorder. Some evenings he would call me to join him, and we would just stand there, watching the sky getting dark as the sun went down behind the opposite building.

At times, Lenny would bring out his typewriter and let me play with it. I would set my fingers in place, and spread them on the keys, like I could type. He would ask me to talk about my ma, like, what she had told me before the accident, or what had happened to me during the lost time, out there on the street. He wanted me to tell all this, not to him—but to his tape recorder.

And once I started, I could say anything—any damn thing—without him cutting in, or getting angry, or making a sound, even.

I would be in a different place then, so far away, as to forget he was there, listening. *Record*. I would talk and talk. And if it was too much for him, Lenny would surprise me by taking himself elsewhere: he would go inside, and sit on the bench, and wait till I was too tired to go on. *Stop*.

After such a night, it would be hard for me to fall asleep. And if I did, I would soon open my eyes with a feeling of dread in my heart, and like, trying to break out of a bad dream. It's always the same dream, too, and it's been coming back, over and again, to haunt me.

Just yesterday—when I laid there in bed, bleeding all day, not even knowing where I was—that was when at last, the dream found me.

In it, I find myself in a public place, which is strange to me—even though I know, somehow, that I've already been here. I've visited this place, perhaps the night before.

It's raised like a stage, and flooded with light: a harsh glare, which blinds me. For a minute I can't see nothing in the dark, beyond that ledge—but I know that them faces are out there, blank and blurry. They're all there, hushing each other, gazing at me.

I see myself standing there in front of them, naked.

Red-faced, I hunch up as tight as I can. I fold over my thighs, trying to hide, to cover my body, my shame—but my hands, they're way too small, so my nipple slips out of my fingers. And there it is, circled by light, for all to see, and to jeer at me, and to lick their lips, which is like, glistening out there, tiny sparks hissing in the distance.

For a little while, my sleep is light. And so—even as I'm looking straight into that spotlight, or like, reaching down to touch the ledge of that stage—I can tell that all this is false, it's nothing more than a dream. But then I fall deeper, even deeper into it, and now I really believe what I see:

Some thread is crawling on my skin. Laying across my knees is a strap of fabric, which is frayed and stained, here and there, with my blood. When I pull it in, trying to drape it around me, or use it for a blanket, it resists. It don't hardly give in, 'cause it's tied to something—no, somebody—standing right here, directly over my bare back.

Me, I don't want to turn, but I take a peek over my shoulder. Wrapped in layers of rags and straps and loose ends, all of which is tattered and like, drenched in reds and browns, the figure seemed shaky. He lifts one leg, and tries to balance himself, teetering—this way and that—on one foot. His hand tries to touch the back of my neck—and misses it, grabbing a handful of air, instead.

And his blood-red lips, they're curled up, in something that looks an awful lot like a smile. A mocking smile, one that don't change.

In my dream, my feet must have frozen. I can't move, can't run away from him, or even climb off the stage, because at that point I'm weak, and too scared to even breathe, and because of that thread, which binds us. And so, rooted to that spot, I look up at him. At this close range, our eyes meet, and my heart skips a beat, 'cause at that second, his are empty.

Suddenly I catch sight of someone else, someone standing way over there, in the distance, behind him; behind the curtains,

even. Except for her hand, which is caught in the light, it's hard
to even notice her, 'cause at first she's like, real shy, even modest,
and keeps herself in the shadows, out of the spotlight.

But then, she changes. Her long fingers, they're gathered, one
by one, into a fist. And twisted around her little finger, you can
find—if you focus—the ends of the rags, and the straps, and the
thread, all of which extend from there to here, where he stands;
all the way, to the joints of his wrists and his elbows, tying them
like, real tight.

And from backstage, she's pulling him—raising, dropping,
tightening, loosening—making the puppet move, shake, jiggle,
even dance on the tip of his toe, and like, bringing him,
somehow, to life. I gasp, thinking: she can twist him around her
little finger, if she wants to.

Me, I cringe as he puffs, breathing something in my ear. "Go,
go back home, go," says the puppet, in a voice that is not really
his. "Go to the place, the place where you came from, you came
from. Go back to your ma, ma, your mama."

And to the sound of teeth gnashing, I force my eyes open, and in
one rip I tear the thread and break out, out of this dream, and
find myself back here, like, in a safe place again.

And the last thing—just before the stage falls away, and things
seem to blur out, and other things become solid, like the ceiling
above my bed, which is finally all clear—the last thing I do is
wonder, is she playing us all? Am I being twisted here, twisted
around her finger, like he is? Am I a puppet, too?

Like, how can I be sure that I'm not?

I wake up. The first thing I do is move, 'cause I ain't frozen
no more. I move them joints—the joints of my own wrists and

elbows—every which way, to make sure I can do it at will. I look at them from this side and that, to check that they ain't tied, or pulled by something, like some blood stained thread.

And the second thing I do is say aloud to myself, "I told you so. I told you so, didn't I?"

My Own Voice

Chapter 8

I'm here, and this is amazing. Crumpled in front of me is his first attempt at telling my story.

Last night was real special for me. He came back from work, and after his son had moped about the place and finally, gone out for a drink or something, which was right after dinner, Lenny stepped out to the balcony, and instead of pressing them keys on the tape recorder, he opened his notebook—the thick one, with the worn cover, which must have seen better days— and said, "Come over here, Anita. Let me read you a little something."

I did. I plopped down and made myself comfortable on his knees.

The page rustled in his hand and he said, "This here, it is one of my early stories," and out of his notebook he started reading, like, *Leonard was first introduced to Lana at his boss's house...*

At once I thought, *Leonard?* Why *Leonard?* The name sounded too important, to formal to my ears. Plain *Lenny* would have been so much better, because after all it was his voice, and the story was clearly about him.

Them writers, sometimes they play these kinds of games, and use code names, I reckon, to distance themselves from themselves.

Anyway, I didn't hardly say anything, 'cause me, I was glad, so glad that this time, he let me in, and here I was, awful close to him. I'd known him, on and off—more off than on—for ten years, and in all that time I'd never, ever heard him read from his notebook for me. Strange: since the beginning he'd been a bit vague about his writing, slippery even. And I didn't mind. No really, I didn't, because... Well, because I accept Lenny. He is what he is: the keeper of secrets.

As it happened, I didn't hear his story last night either. This time, it was my fault. Right after the first few words I relaxed, and felt so at ease, and so warm inside, that I caught myself yawning.

My head lolled to one side, then another, and I think I dozed off—but anyway, Lenny didn't mind this time, not at all, "Because," he said, "it must be because you are pregnant. And the bleeding, too, must take a lot out of you."

He let me slip off his knees, and then moved aside so I could share the seat with him. "Your eyes," he said, "they are glazing over. Lean on me, right here. My God, Anita, you look so pale, so tired. Well, who can blame you?"

Which was kinda good, 'cause he didn't have a clue that it wasn't just me being pregnant, and tired, and what not—but on top of everything else, it was his writing, and all them words, the fine words he used, which confused me and made me drowsy.

Lenny was like, delighted by his own writing, and by me being there, silent, without butting in, because according to him Natasha, his ex-wife, had laughed at him more than once, in the early years, the years of her success, during which he was out of a job. He hadn't forgotten the insult, but managed to swallow it, somehow—only to spit it out now, so many years later. She would say, like, Who does he think he is, Dostoyevsky?

Unlike her I just clung to him, and took in the moment, and tried to listen, as best I could, first hearing the sound of his voice and then, deep inside, the throbbing of my heart.

And then... Then I closed my eyes.

When I woke up—it must have been long after midnight—he was still reading, jotting down notes, erasing, and from time to time, pressing this or that key on the tape recorder. And he was talking, talking to me or, perhaps, to himself. *Rewind, Play. Play, Rewind.*

I propped my head up on his shoulder and looked up at his mouth, and the little muscles at play all around it, which didn't look near as tight as they've been, say, in the past few days. I could see that something had come over him: something even stronger than his passion to write. A great relief, that's what it was. Like, a load had been taken off his heart.

I bet it happened when he gave up his secret to me, the one secret he guarded most of all, which was funny, 'cause it wasn't even his—but Natasha's.

Now that I knew about her illness I felt kinda dizzy in my head. Like, I was playing with danger, soaring, even hovering in midair, over the high side of a teeter-totter, and spotting Natasha over there, on the opposite side. By some twist, our fate was like, linked. This time around, her luck was down, mine—up. I could sense the shock, the deep fall she'd taken, and the hard hit against the ground.

And I figured that now, she didn't barely have a way to come back. She wasn't a threat no more.

Meanwhile, Lenny went on scribbling. His right arm was holding the pen, his left—hugging me, which was cool. The night air was swirling around us. I watched the setting of the moon as it flowed down, so slow—so magical, even—till it fell away behind the outline of the next building. A star here, a star there gave a faint glint. Time slowed down, like, by some spell. I had goosebumps, 'cause I couldn't remember no moment but now, and no place but here, when I felt peace, complete peace between us.

And after a long while I caught the hint, the first hint of dawn, and I touched him, with nothing, nothing at all coming between us—not even that thing, whatever it was, Dostoyevsky.

I can't remember how he took me to bed. By the time I got up this morning, Lenny was already gone.

So now, it's a new day.

I go out to the balcony, listening for echoes from last night, like, echoes of me and Lenny. First I try to *Rewind, Play*. Then I *Stop*, and try instead to bring them voices out of memory. I prick up my ears for anything, any little thing that's still here, still left from that charm, that moment of pure calm—but no: all's quiet, quiet in the most regular, humdrum way, with a distant buzz of street noises.

It's late in the morning, which you can tell, 'cause the dew on the railing has dried up by now. His desk is bare, not even a pen left here, on the glass surface. And on the floor, a film of dust has already covered our footprints, so it's awful hard to believe that last night really happened, that it wasn't just another dream.

His notebook is nowhere in sight—but then, under his desk, right there in the trashcan, I can see a bunch of papers peeking out over the edge. I take them out, and smooth the edges, and try to flatten the creases, and blot out the ink stains.

According to him, only one of his stories was published, like, ages ago. The rest of them wasn't, on account of the fact that Lenny don't send them to no magazine editors, because, he says, he isn't quite finished improving a phrase here and there, and besides, most of them stories, they're just too private. So the more he tells you, the more he seems to leave something out.

Here, look: the first page is kinda messy. It's that story, the one he managed to publish, the one he read for me last night. Me, I can barely recall what it is I've heard. I think it's about a girl, a girl with blond streaks in her hair. Lana.

To win her over, a man can be seduced to do just about anything, and like, give up the one thing about himself which he values the most. Now as far as Lenny goes, I'm way too easy, which means, this girl isn't me. And for sure, she isn't Natasha.

Not long ago Lenny told me, "My writing is not the place where the fiction is," which I find strange, 'cause if not in his stories—then, where else can his fiction be? Is he writing the truth—and living a falsehood? If this is so, then the girl from his story must be real. More real than me, anyway.

Whoever she is, she must be someone he'd known way back in the past. I don't think he's seeing her now. I really don't.

Then again, I may be totally wrong: perhaps the only place where she exists is like, on paper, which explains why he didn't barely give her a strong, clear voice. To me, she seems a bit sketchy. In six pages of dense scribbles, the only line he let her say is like, *What is it with you tonight?*

With him, every little thing is huge—or else he's gonna make it so. And every gesture—even as trivial as a wink—can be a trigger, like, for a whole big drama, which may be the case here, in this story. I'm gonna read it later. I have time. At least, I think I do.

Here's another crumpled page, which is nearly empty—except for a single sentence, parts of which is crossed out. Between the scratches, it reads:

He's gone, but still, I'm thinking about him, about how he has touched on that time, the lost time nearly five years ago, when I went out the door, swearing I won't come back to him, not ever. What he hasn't said—and what left such a bitter taste in my mouth—is how he told me, back then, You are a nice kid. Go, go back to where you came from. Go back to your mama.

These are my words—not his.

I'm so surprised to find them here, suddenly on paper. I bet he hit *Rewind, Rewind, Rewind* and ended up going back more than he'd intended, which is how he found what I'd said on tape that night, when I couldn't fall asleep, on account of that nightmare.

I reckon he listened. Yes. He did.

Now I ain't sure how I feel about that. Part of me is glad; the other, not so much. I take the page with me, 'cause like, even if it's in his hand—or maybe because of it—this a part of me, of who I am.

And I go inside, into the living room, and sit there, on the piano bench, and lay my head on the surface, which covers the keyboard of the piano, which is kinda cool to the touch. And then I dream.

I dream about Lenny: How he's gonna come home this evening, and ask me to tell him something again, about myself, and about things I remember, things I'm painting in my head. After a while he's gonna go away, leaving me alone with the tape recorder.

Record. Stop.

Once my story is done, he's gonna come back to take some notes, and edit them over and again, scratching and erasing all night long, and like, going into the trouble of finding a way— just the right way—to carry my voice in letters, and in marks.

I reckon it won't easy for him to fix the way I talk—and at the same time, remain true to how I tell it, and to the feel, the real feel of how it happened.

I can just see Lenny in my head: He's gonna torture himself trying, somehow, to do it, so that tomorrow morning, at exactly the same time, when I'm gonna be sitting here again, on this very bench, I'm gonna be startled to find—out there on his desk —a gift.

A little something from him to me: A little piece of paper, scribbled side to side, top to bottom, with dense writing, and barely a space between the words.

As usual, it would seem as if he's sucked up all them spaces, because—even when he gives—Lenny don't really want you to get it. Or else, he wants you to work hard at getting it.

And even then, he wants you to figure out only small parts, some here, some there. Any which way, it won't help him. I'm gonna get it, 'cause them spaces, and the lack of them, may be his—but the words are mine.

I'm gonna snatch the paper, and find myself blown away, 'cause right there—in his hand, black on white—I'm gonna read the scrawl, the words of my voice, my own voice:

I'm here, and this is amazing.

And then:

Crumpled in front of me is his first attempt at telling my story.

Above All, Survival

Chapter 9

I don't know how we got to this place, Lenny and me, and I don't really care to know. Let's just say that what's happening between us isn't exactly clear. Yes, let's leave it at that. At first I tried to tell myself he won't touch me because of the pregnancy. I refused to admit that the heat between us had been cooling off even before that—but now, like, there's no warmth left here no more.

Like ma used to say, when she called her customers to offer her usual special—I mean, the three dollar palm reading special —she said, "No, really? No warmth left? Trust me, it just looks that way—till you touch them embers. Red hot passion like that, it can't never die out. But see, it can change its color and blacken him inside, and like, turn to hate, or contempt, or jealousy."

"You better be careful," she said, "'cause when you least expect it, it's gonna flare out again."

Which forces me to take a hard look at where I stand, and like, avoid wasting time dreaming, or wondering about matters of the heart, fluid matters which may take me nowhere in a hurry, and which no one—not even ma—can't never predict. I have a hunch that I must be real careful now, and stop acting on a hunch.

From now on I'm gonna knock myself out doing something totally different, like planning every one of my next moves.

At this point there's one worry which is, like, blocking everything else in my head, and this is it: I've fainted once, I may faint again. So I can't go on alone. And even if I could, I shouldn't, really.

I must find someone here I can trust, someone willing to hold my hand and steady me, in case I'm too weak to stand straight. I don't give a damn what this someone thinks of me. I swear I can take it, 'cause now that I'm pregnant, it's more than just me. My little one is curled here inside me. I must take care of him. That's all that matters. I so wish ma was here. Without her, the place I'm gonna hear the sound—the sweet sound of my baby's heartbeat—is gonna be among strangers.

With her gone, where can I go? To whom shall I turn? Don't laugh, even if—on the surface—my solution may seem absurd, totally absurd to you. I reckon I must win the trust of the women in this family, which is to say them Rosenblatt sisters, armed with their knitting needles, and spearheaded by dear old aunt Hadassa.

At the time I told her not to trouble herself with coming to my wedding, and to stay as far as she could from me, which may have been the wrong thing to say to the old witch—but boy did it feel right!

You may think me crazy, totally crazy to even consider her. And maybe I am, 'cause how can I forget: it was aunt Hadassa who came up with that bright idea, the idea of abortion. With the sweetest fake smile you could imagine, she told me that for sure, there was still time, it wasn't too late to have it, and like, it could make things so, so much easier for me, because the way she sees it, I like to run around, and have my fun and stuff.

So right there and then I had the best fun I'd had in a long while: it was like, such a pleasure for me to let her have it! I swear, I was rude as hell! I shouted at her with such goddam delight, so she would know who's who in this place, 'cause guess what: the future of this family is right here, in my womb. Now don't you forget it!

But from now on I must swallow my pride—even if it chokes me to death. I must hold my tongue with them sisters, and like, be nice, and show respect, which isn't gonna be easy for me, 'cause you can look far and wide—but for sure, you can't find no witches more uglier than them.

I remind myself: above all, survival. So I must do something to turn them around, somehow, from hating me. I must, like, charm them into thinking of my baby as one of their own— even if to them, I'm always gonna remain the stranger.

Me, I'm used to being the enemy, but if they know what's good for them, they're gonna come around real soon and make peace.

It's in my power to bring them out of that slow death—that endless, idle boredom of old age, and make them come alive again, the way it must have been for them back then, twenty-seven years ago, when Ben was a newborn baby.

I can just picture them spinsters, crowding around the crib, fat bellies hanging over the little wool blanket, trying to walk on tiptoe, stepping over each other's warts, and carrying a bucket load of free advice, for which they wasn't even asked, let alone thanked, 'cause you see, there he was, so, so frail, and always crying it seemed.

So they must have wondered, like, was the little bundle of joy hungry or wet or sleepy, or was he just too cold or warm or sick or something. I can just see it in my head. They would tell his mama to burp him, and to clean his little tush and powder it—even though the three of them hadn't taken care of one, I mean, not even once in their life.

And Natasha, she must have been close to tears, 'cause like, being new to being a new mama, I bet she wasn't sure if she'd done things right, and she couldn't tell if there was enough milk in her breasts, 'cause like, the baby won't stop wailing. And them nipples, I'm sure they was hurting like hell.

It would be just like aunt Hadassa to say that if she was in Natasha's place—which thank God, she wasn't—she would ignore the pain. My, my, she would say, never mind a little discomfort, because you know, breast feeding is not for sissies, dear.

And she won't back down, I'm sure—even though the three of them hadn't done nothing even slightly close to anything of the sort.

And when all that advice won't do much in the way of calming the baby down, they would tell Natasha that it was fine, just ignore the crying, because anyway, it was meant to make his lungs strong and healthy—even though aunt Hadassa had to stuff her big ears with a couple of cotton wads, 'cause in spite of her own advice, I bet she couldn't stand hearing it no more.

Now I could make her feel needed again. I could even stun her, by inviting her right in, to meddle in my affairs in full view; which is what I did last night, when I couldn't take that noise in my head no more, I mean the old alarm clock, out there in the hall, which had become awful pesky with that loud tick-tock, tick-tock.

First I switched the light off, and held my hand just under the bulb to feel the air cooling off, and sat there in the darkening kitchen for a quite a long while, trying to amuse myself by touching my belly, and thinking about my baby, and about his future, about the long years ahead, which helped me tune out the minutes, ticking away.

Then I stood back up, trying to find my reflection, which looked real small and buckled right there, on the round surface of that black bulb. I wiped my tears—even though I didn't have no sleeves on me—after which I went to the hall and piled some papers and stuff, right on top of the alarm clock, to muffle that sound.

Then I called her up, and said, like, "Aunt Hadassa, I need you—"

"What for?" she said, real cautious.

And I said, "I have an appointment, like, tomorrow at ten—"

And she said, "You do, dear? Nu, what for?"

And by the acid tone in her voice I figured she was thinking that by now, it was too late anyway, and that I should've listened to her when there was still time, time for a proper abortion, because my, my, now it was week number twelve already.

So I said, "It's a real surprise, aunt Hadassa. You'll see. Anyway, let me ask you this: can you come here, like, early tomorrow morning, and help me get ready?"

And she answered by asking, "You not feeling well?"

And I had to say, "No, not that well, Aunt Hadassa."

"My, my," she clicked her tongue. "I'll be there, dear. We all will."

"I'm awful glad," I said, and meant it. "Don't know what I would do without you."

And I thought, In a few months from now, I'm gonna steal her heart. Aunt Hadassa is gonna feel, like, the grip of a little hand around her wrinkled finger. She's gonna pinch a chubby little cheek, and listen for a thin, ringing voice calling her name. And me, I'm gonna smile at her, and place my baby right there, in her lap, and watch her droopy eyes light up. She's gonna know that I know that she knows that from now on she owes me, 'cause like, I can make her feel wanted again, which is a mighty strong thing to feel.

It's in my power. Without having to say any of it, it's gonna be awful clear to both of us.

Up to now she hasn't give it much thought—but with a little help from me, she will. And then, then she'll change. She'll be *my* aunt—the stolen aunt Hadassa—whether she knows it at this point, or not.

I can't wait till tomorrow. I bet I ain't gonna forget the place where—for the first time—I'll hear the sound, the sweet sound of my baby's heartbeat. Only I wonder now, like, Will it be among strangers.

The Heartbeat

Chapter 10

In spite of the light spotting I refused to admit to myself, even for one moment, how terribly worried I really was. Lenny didn't come back, so all alone in the big bed I felt lost, like I was drowning, and had to hold my breath, somehow, till dawn, and then even longer, till the light of day, till my ten o'clock appointment, because I was so afraid I was gonna get some bad news, I mean, about my little one.

So now I pinch myself, 'cause at long last it's ten already, and here I am, in a half-darkened office, lying on my back, waiting, like, for a miracle, straining to hear a sound—which isn't here, isn't here yet—the sound of my baby's heartbeat. If something's wrong then it's time, time to find out.

With a heavy sigh, a woman in her mid-thirties takes a seat right here facing me. She types my name, so that now, *'Anita Kaminsky'* shines above me in large letters on a screen.

If not for her red eyes, and them sharply pointed ears, she would seem the perfect clinical type. Her thin mouth is pursed pretty tight, except to let out, kinda under her breath, that she's sick of all this, and who cares, nobody gives a damn, and really why should they, it's her life, and her problem is no one else's business, and to call her Debbie, she's a *sonographer*, and this plastic thing, this gismo she's gripping in her hand, that's called a probe. With that she begins sliding it around the bottom of my belly.

I hold very still. I don't barely move under that crisp, starched sheet. It has ironed pleats that stay there, like, straight as an arrow, even when it's spread open, right here over my legs.

Her movement is measured, precise—but all the same, I reckon my baby's squirming inside, because of all that prodding. It tickles me, too. I'm afraid I'm gonna pee in my panties, because that probe thing which is resting here, on my skin, feels kinda wet, kinda cool to the touch. For her, I bet all this is just routine. Me, I have to hold a full bladder, which isn't easy—but then, then the beat starts!

It sounds faint at first, just like nothing, and then all of a sudden it grows awful strong. Now that she's found it, and it blips loud and clear, the smile can't hardly be wiped off my face. If not for them red eyes, I would've asked her, like, if I was to come back the next day, would she let me listen again.

If not for them three witches standing there in the corner squinting at me—perhaps even wishing me ill—I would've lost all sense of shame: I would've cried and cried, and then cried some more. It's the most sweet, beautiful sound I've ever heard in my entire life!

But never mind me, or how I feel. You can see straight away that the most amazing change is beginning to take place right over there, out of that corner, when all three of them—aunt Hadassa, aunt Frida and aunt Fruma—come forward, like, in one heavy step, which makes the floor bounce right under me. I've taken a risk asking them to come here with me, and I hope, I so hope it won't prove to be no mistake.

I reckon they hate me, 'cause from the beginning, from the time I fainted they've been hinting that this here pregnancy, it don't seem to be viable, and it should be aborted, and there's still time, like, to do it. Still, there's no one else to offer a helping hand, no one else to lean on, in case I'm gonna feel dizzy again. From now on, hate don't really matter no more, 'cause I need them.

Blip, blip, blip goes the sound, and them three aunts, they pop their round, bulging eyes and lean right over my belly, which is glistening in the dark with that clear gel smear, in which the probe thing is like, splashing around. And aunt Hadassa, she raises her painted eyebrows, and screws up her nose till it's glued to the screen, like she hasn't seen nothing like that in her entire life, which I bet, she hasn't.

Me, I thought I knew what to expect. From the book Lenny gave me I've learned that at week twelve, the baby's fingers would soon begin to open and close. His toes would curl, his eye muscles would clench, and his mouth would make sucking movements.

By now his eyes have already moved from the sides of his head to the front, and his ears is like, right there where they should be. I thought I could see all that in my head—but for sure, it isn't hardly the same as watching the real thing, 'cause the real thing is like, much more confusing.

"See, right here?" says the sonographer.

And I say, "No, what?"

And she points out, "The heartbeat, see? Down here, across the monitor?"

So I turn to the screen, which is as black as night, and fix my eyes on that white worm, which is radiating there, all the way across, with them shining spikes pulsing through it, one blip after another, running off at the right edge and then, coming right back in at the left one.

"Sure," I say, real bold, like I know what I'm talking about. "The heartbeat."

"Yes," she says, like we have a clear meeting of the minds between us. "This here, that's what you call a Doppler waveform, see? And it shows the systoles and diastoles in the blood flow velocity."

"Looks good," I say.

"For you," she says, "the important thing is this: Even in the presence of vaginal bleeding, which is what you have, we can depict a visible heartbeat. So obviously, the fetus is viable."

Here she lets me take a deep breath, and then goes on to say, "It means that the probability of a continued pregnancy is better than 95 percent."

"Looks good, awful good," I say again.

And from behind, them three witches mumble, "Nu? Looks good, doesn't it."

And they turn back to retreat into that corner, from where I can still hear them, whispering, "My, my," and clicking their tongue from time to time.

Meanwhile she freezes the image and prints a little picture for me, so that later I can show the little worm to my husband. Right this minute I ain't all that sure I want to do that.

She turns a few knobs, and pushes a few sliders and stuff on her keyboard, so a pale search light appears in the image. It's scanning around some dusky nooks and crannies, where silvery, flat layers—some thin, some thick—have sunk down into the dark, just like wet mud. It isn't barely clear to me that what I see up there is for real. Perhaps the light just flashes there, off the sludge, and what it mirrors back to me is like, false. Something just dreamed up.

The ray flutters about, slicing, somehow, across them layers of dense, grainy clay of what's inside me. At first I don't much mind all that slicing, 'cause it don't hurt me, and it don't feel like nothing, really.

With a soft, squelching sound, little specs glitter in the dark fluid. And there—just behind them specs—something moves! Something catches the light and like, wow! For a second there I can swear I see a hand: My baby's hand waving, then turning to float away.

This isn't exactly what I've expected, 'cause like, not only is that fluid kinda see-through—but to my surprise, so is the little hand. Like, you can spot not only the faint outline of flesh on them, but the shine of the bones coming at you, too.

Me, I'm here to protect my baby, to keep him safe from harm, even from the shadow of harm. So I tell her, "Now, stop that!"

And she points her ears even sharper, saying, "Excuse me?"

So I go, real slow, I say, "You heard me. Turn the damn thing off."

And them three aunts, they stop whispering amongst themselves. Right away they click their heels, like, awful hard against the floor to rise up, and aunt Hadassa says Oy, which is quickly echoed, like, Oy Oy, by aunt Fruma and aunt Frida. Anyhow, they seem eager to find out what it is I'm fussing about.

So I insist, this time much louder, "Stop, stop already! You slicing my baby!"

And the sonographer, she freezes the image, and tries to hold me off, saying, like, "Ultrasound scan only looks like a slice through the flesh, but trust me, it isn't."

And in turn I ask, "Is it fake, then?"

"Listen," she tells me, with a tone that is half-polite, half-tired, half-annoyed, "it's considered to be a safe, non invasive, accurate and cost-effective investigation in the fetus, and not to worry."

Here she glances, with some caution, at them aunts, 'cause by now they've come awful close to the screen, which is where she, the sonographer, stands, if you can call that standing, 'cause really she's leaning back ever so slightly, like, away from them.

"None of you fine women should worry in the least," she says. "As you may already know, ultrasound has become an indispensable obstetric tool, which plays an important role in the care of every pregnant woman. My job here is to take some measurements, which reflect the gestational age of the fetus, to arrive at the correct dating of birth—"

"All right," I cut in, 'cause by now I've figured that despite all this rattling, she means well.

Still, I'm glaring at her, like, to stop her from chattering, 'cause anyway she don't barely make any sense. "Go on, then," I tell her, "go on with them measurements, but from now on, you better be real careful."

In reply she mumbles something, making the mistake of thinking that from where I lie, I can't see her rolling her eyeballs, which seem, somehow, even redder than before. So just to make myself clear I spell things out for her, like, "We don't want to see no more slicing, you hear?"

She blinks, giving a slight nod to me, which means that at last, we have a clear understanding between us fine women.

The image comes alive, and there is that black bubble again, swimming in in its gravy. She marks an outer edge around it, which at once, brings it so close to you that like, it could almost swallow you.

And in it you can spot, yes, you can suddenly find—gleaming there, in and out from them fuzzy, gnarly shadows—the most beautiful side view of a baby:

My little one curled there on his back, like he's just about to start bouncing around. There, there's his face! He's bathed in light, with a round forehead and plump cheek and the cutest little nose you've ever seen. And there's his lips, which is like, gulping for air, the mouth opening, closing on his own little thumb and then, sucking it.

Aunt Hadassa drops her chin in surprise, and in spite of trying her best to contain herself, she gives a shrill little yelp, after which the sonographer tells her, like, Enough! And to leave the office at once, because she's had it already, up to here!

And with a sigh, she warns us that she may quit her job right now, right in the middle of this here session, because God knows how she's even managed to make it to work this morning. She's so broken-hearted after last night, which was when—without no warning—her husband got up and left her, because she'd tried and tried but no matter how hard she kept on trying, she couldn't get pregnant.

By now she's like, on a roll: She can't stop herself from talking to me, even though she don't pay no attention to how I'm twisting here, on them fresh sheets, and how I'm biting my lips, which I have to do, 'cause I need to pee so bad, I really need to go, like, right now.

But what can I do? She isn't a sonographer no more, just plain Debbie, who talks and blinks, blinks and talks to no end, telling me how he turned, for just a second, and looked back at her over his shoulder, perhaps waiting for her to beg him to stay —but in sheer despair she cried out, Well? Don't just stand there —go! Go already! And so, finally, he did.

I can see she's in pain, and she don't need no advice from me, 'cause my man isn't no better anyhow, and who knows what to expect of him now. So I raise myself on my elbow and lean closer and touch her arm to say, like, I'm so, so sorry for you, Debbie. So now she starts sobbing, she's in tears, which at least stops her from blinking all the time. She says she can't take it no more, like, looking at them fetuses sucking their stubby little thumbs all day long.

And her parents, she says, they come from the old country, where a divorced woman's no better than damaged goods, so of course she isn't gonna tell them nothing about all this, because like, what will they say? She would much rather talk to a stranger—someone she won't see no time soon—or just bury it all inside.

Then Debbie wipes her swollen eyes to stare at aunt Hadassa, and to say that this screaming, right in her ears, makes her nervous, because she's in a delicate state, which you can tell by the sound of her hiccups and from time to time, her sniveling.

Her hand, she says, may turn shaky, which is a sign of bad luck, because that would prevent her from taking them measurements, such as the Crown Rump Length around the head, right here on screen, and the Femur Length, and the

Abdominal Circumference, all of which requires great focus and like, complete silence around her.

So without a word aunt Hadassa hangs her head, and beats a path of retreat across the floor, like a wise, old general knowing when to admit defeat on the battlefield. Her two sisters march out the door closely behind her, and together they all wait for me outside. I can hear them whispering excitedly to each other.

When Debbie is finally done getting herself together and taking all them measurements, she tells me to go empty my bladder, which is a lucky thing, 'cause at this point I'm ready to burst, like, before you can even finish saying *sonographer*.

Then I get out to the waiting room, eager to get out as quick as I can, to find out if Lenny's come back home. Along the way I'm trying to put my hands in the sleeves of my winter coat and buckle my pink belt around me—only to discover that it don't fit me no more, 'cause my body, it isn't barely as slim as I thought it was.

Looking down on it, a view comes to me in a flash, which makes me brace myself, like, for danger: Down there on the floor, aiming at me from left, right and center, is the sharp, pointed tips, the tips of three pairs of shoes.

Me, I look up, and can't barely believe what I see: Aunt Hadassa gives me a smile, as do her sisters. "Wait, don't just go," she says, in the most disarming manner. "Stand there!"

Gone is the acid tone in her voice. Gone is that squint of suspicion. Them witches, they look awful friendly this time around. At first I figure that having seen my baby, they simply have no choice but to glow, just because of adoring him—but like, it's a bit more than that.

"My God, you are fearless!" says aunt Hadassa. "I dare say, you are just like me."

"No," I tell her, "I'm tougher."

"A fighter, is what you are! I mean, you would kill to keep your baby safe."

To which I say, "You bet I would."

Then, seeing me feel around my belt, like, to find the next hole in it, Aunt Hadassa offers, "Here, let me help you with that, dear."

And she draws even closer, and wraps herself around me— mushy, droopy flesh flapping like wings under her arms—and clicks my belt into place, so now it hangs nice and loose around my waist.

Then she takes a step back, letting me lead the way out, which is when I know that she knows that there's no way I'm gonna let no one stop me.

No one—I swear—no one can draw this story to a close, by telling me there's still time, like, to end it.

This is week twelve. My pregnancy's viable, and it's not to be aborted. So now, as we walk out, we fine women peer straight into each other's eyes, knowing that at long last, we have a clear meeting of the minds between us.

The Naked Bulb

Chapter 11

Since the bleeding began, I've been missing my ma more and more. If she was here I could ask her, like, How come I feel so alone. How come I can see, all of a sudden I can now see how my youth is wasting away in this place. Like, I have no air, I'm wilting here. And Lenny, he don't even pay no attention, 'cause he's back to his usual thing, which is: comb his thinning, gray hair—sleek it back, real slow and careful—and then work all day, write all night, either out or away.

Me, I thought getting married was meant to change things— but then, if things are changing it's not for the better.

It's funny how now—when she's out of my reach forever—I feel so close, so terribly close to her. At least now, ma don't push me back no more. She can't say, like, Enough, girl! Snap out of it! And she don't get in the way, I mean, in the way of me doing what I've been wishing for so long I could do, which is just cling, cling real close to her. I so miss the smell of her face: a mix of sweat, cheap eau de cologne and cigarette smoke. I try to dream up that smell, which gags me, and stings my eyes, and brings me close to tears.

If she was here I could ask her, like, when did she have the hunch, the first clear hunch that pa was gonna leave us, and how long after that did it happen.

At this point I don't know how much longer I can go on relying on Lenny, 'cause even when he's here, even when he fixes his eyes on me, there's something in them lately, something hard, even furious, which I swear, I don't really get.

Last night I was so worried—worried to the point of getting mad—because for some reason, Lenny didn't come home at all, even though I got all ready for him, all prettied up with my little black dress, which for the first time I had trouble zipping up, 'cause my belly had just started to grow, and to get rounder than it used to be.

He wasn't there—but to me, it felt like he could watch me through them walls. I felt choked. I even cussed him in my heart. I told myself it was just a dumb, crazy feeling, and to stop fighting for a breath. Still, it felt like Lenny could spot, somehow, the sudden blush that—in spite of myself—started flaming on my skin, the moment I passed by kitchen and laid eyes on his son.

In a blink, the air felt steaming hot all around me.

This was something new to me, 'cause up to this moment I didn't exactly care for Ben—even though from this angle, the slant of his shoulders looked just the same as his pa's. Suddenly my heart went pit-a-pat, which—I swear—didn't happen never before. If my husband was here tonight, if he hadn't left me, it won't have happened now. No matter how much I tried to cool it, here I was, blushing, on account of the fact that I've just blushed.

And Ben, he was leaning back, lost in his dreams in the corner. His pale face and his mussed up hair fell just outside the light, the dim, fuzzy light which had no border, no clear border anywhere on the kitchen table, 'cause there wasn't no lampshade over the bulb, on account of the fact it had been broken and removed, like, ages ago, and never replaced.

I bet you would have me turn away, which was the right thing to do—but it was already too late, so I didn't. Anyway, I could already tell that Ben could tell, by the swish of my hair, that there I was, just about to cross the threshold. His nostrils flared up, like, to breathe in the scent, the faint scent of my shampoo, mingled with a dab of perfume.

I could've walked past that door—but then, this I knew: whatever happened, in your eyes it would always be my fault. The boy wants me. He wants me real bad, and for that, I pity him. He would soon kill himself if he can't have me—but any which way, you would blame it on me. In your eyes, the boy can't be nothing else than naive. So of course, it must've been me, me who seduced him.

You would call me a bad girl—so then, why shouldn't I be?

For ten years I tried, as best I could, to be squeaky clean. It's too damn hard, and you don't never trust me anyway. So instead I could really go wild, and take my revenge on my husband, by giving him a reason—a *real* reason this time—to be jealous, so he don't need to go searching for one.

I beg you, Lenny, I whispered. Come back to me, or else... From this point on, things won't be the same, never again. I swear, I'm gonna do something bad, gonna hurt you, dear, so you won't never leave me like this, without even saying one word.

After a while I dried my eyes. Hell, what's the point praying, or hoping, or threatening, when anyhow, you ain't even here to listen.

So I came in, hips swaying, and looked down at the boy, saying, "Help me, Ben."

Which startled him. The features of his face contorted, like he couldn't make up his mind whether to be troubled by me surprising him, or not.

Either way, he sprang to his feet and with a shaky voice, said, "Sure, what—"

And I turned my back on him, and tugged at the zipper of my black dress, pulled it as high as it would go, so now it reached the level of my waist, and then I just stood there, waiting for him to make his move. And with trembling fingers Ben brought the two edges of fabric together—barely touching the back of my neck—and managed, somehow, to pull the thing all the way up.

"There," he said, with a catch in his voice. "It is done."

And then he stepped back, away from me. I reckon he was thinking about the late hour, and about his pa, who should've been here already, and about not being able to face him, 'cause like, how can you try to rob the old man of his woman, and how can you win any fight—let alone dare to stay in it—while having to carry, somehow, the terrible handicap of being young.

I licked my lips, so they would be real red and shiny, and smiled at him. Inside I was praying that the light in the bulb would blaze so bright, so fiery it would burst. And them walls, pressing awful tight all around us, would just melt away. And the pane of glass would sizzle, and the window frame, it would turn to ashes—poof!—like dust into thin air, so anyone out there in the street could watch us, as if there wasn't no walls, and we didn't have no shelter. Then there would be no secrets no more. Nothing left to hide.

Here, Lenny, I cried inside, take a good look! Here I am—not only for your eyes, but for all eyes to see!

And for the first time in our ten years together I thought, he's old. He's the old man passing out there, somewhere in the dark, limping stiffly on his way to some other woman, some fake blond, I bet. At the sound of my voice he would shiver, and look up. He would be unable to take his eyes off the boy. And the boy, he would just freeze there, in his seat, unable to take his eyes off me.

I hoped, with every bit of bitterness, that Lenny won't miss the look, the shy look his son flashed at me, when I slid into my chair and—real slow and naughty—began crossing my legs.

Which at once, made Ben tense up. I met his eyes, and could feel my look shooting through him, like it was a poisoned arrow. Now my legs was crossed knee on knee, and my lips was wet and parted, ever so slightly, and I began lowering my eyelids. Slowly his face dimmed, like, it fell into a black nothing, and then, I went back to thinking about Lenny:

As a husband, he may lose his temper with me, from time to time—but as a writer, he totally gets what I need. He lets me talk, talk, talk for hours on end, keeping himself out of the way, like, real nice and discreet, so as not to stop me from pouring my heart out in front of his tape recorder.

Me, I put my faith in him, knowing that Lenny would keep his word, he won't listen to nothing I say, 'cause some words, they rattle in your head, and their sound, it can be jolting to anyone, I mean, anyone but you, because they're yours. So you should hide them real good, keep them hushed up, like, under a blanket. Them words, they shouldn't be heard by no one— especially not those you hold dear.

Which makes me trust the distance between us. It keeps me safe—but at the same time, it holds us apart.

So at this moment—when I started punishing him by raising my eyes, and giving Ben that which he craved, a cruel little smile—the best thing that could happen would be this: Lenny would come bursting in.

I can just see it in my head. He would be breathing hot fume straight into my eyes, making me step back and blink. His forehead would be, like, swollen with rage. And that pleat in its middle, which used to remind me of my pa, would grow deeper than ever. And the vein by the side of his neck would seem to be knotted. With an awful screech Lenny would shove the table off to the side, and flick the naked bulb hanging over its place, till it swung violently to and fro, to and fro.

To his son I bet he would say nothing, 'cause if he did—if he said, like, *Stop*! Stop staring at her, she's fucking mine!—things could soon come to blows. Instead, he would just fix his eyes on Ben, scaring him right out of the kitchen. Then, not being able to hold himself back no longer, Lenny would like, explode. He would rip my dress in two and shout at me, and I would shout back, even cry. And then, then it would be all over.

The air would be cleared between us, and we could start fresh, almost.

I should be so lucky—but no; sadly, that didn't happen. Instead I raised my hand—like I was him—and pushed the table, and flicked the naked bulb. Under it—right there between the boy and me—stood Lenny's chair. It looked so empty, so bare that it glowed, like, real bright against the shadows.

There was a splotch of light that danced over the seat, like a dance of triumph, almost. It darted wildly from one edge of the seat to the other, and after a while it started slowing down, swinging only a bit, then only a tiny bit, till at last it stopped right there, right in the center. At which time I felt a little something, a little pang in my heart. Perhaps, remorse.

All the while, Ben went on sitting there, in his chair, pretty stiff and silent. He lowered his head, like, to study his own hands, so as not to stare at me. Nothing else stirred. Me, I glanced out the window: nothing stirred out there, either. You couldn't spot no one in the twilight—but in my head I pictured the old man turning away from me, and in that second I sensed his heart turning, turning against me.

Which is when I snapped my fingers, right there in front of my face, and told myself in a sharp voice, a voice that wasn't even mine, Enough already! Snap out of it, girl!

What's the matter with you, anyway? So, your man hasn't come home? Too bad, really! Who knows where the hell he is. Who cares with whom he's sleeping tonight. Jealousy is a tough thing, Anita. It's taken a bite out of you. It hurts. Yes, I can see the pain. So now, he hasn't come home—and the thing you worry about is *what*, exactly? Crossing your legs? Really? You out of your mind?

I slapped my own cheek thinking, I so wish ma was here.

She Deserves Better

Chapter 12

It's awful nippy here, inside and out, even though this is only mid-fall. Shut tight in front of me is the glass door, which I can't hardly open, on account of being tired, and a bit wobbly on my feet. Even so I can hear a sound, a muffled sound from the other side, out there on the balcony. From this angle I can spot him, kinda: at least his outline, bent over the desk, and the slant of the shoulders.

And I can't barely see a face, but somehow I can tell it's a familiar voice out there, saying, like, *Here is one thing I hope she knows: she deserves better.*

Which makes me shiver, even in my coat. The man, he's tapping his fingers tensely on the edge of the record player, pressing one key, then another, which brings up the voice saying, louder now, *She deserves better,* and again, *deserves better,* then, *better.*

That voice, it's Ben's voice—but them fingers, they're the old man's fingers. The instant he hits *Pause* is when my doubts go away, and like, I know who it is.

So I don't even need him to turn around, and I don't even want to ask him, like, Where was you, 'cause I don't want to hear no lies, and no long stories either, and above all, I tell him in my heart, I don't want to admit how lonely I am here, in this place, which isn't my home, Lenny, without you.

Still absorbed in his work with his back to me, he tries to slide open a drawer, a drawer which I haven't noticed in his desk before—not even the other day, when I went through the jumble of his papers, looking for clues, any clues of where Lenny had gone, or with whom he might be staying, or how he expected me to pay all them bills, because, like ma used to say, money don't come cheap.

I hope he finds things in place now, still in the right state of disorder. I hope I didn't mess up no pages of his writing—or else, his stories will make even less sense than they already do.

The drawer is damn clunky. It rattles a bit under his hand, like, the slides under it must have gotten rusty. Then it comes to a full stop, hanging in midair. He leans in to put his hand right there, inside the mouth of it, and his fingers are swallowed up by a deep shadow, which kinda scares me, like I've seen all this before, in a dream or a movie or something.

So in distress I gulp for air, just about to cry out to him, Stop! Pull out, Lenny! Your hand—no, don't talk, don't even breathe a word—it's about to be bitten off, like, if you don't hold your tongue, right now, hold it from telling me a lie.

Which is the moment he freezes, like he's just caught a sound, the light sound of my footfall. There's a chill in the air, which I can see right here, in front of my nose, 'cause like, the vapor of my breath starts rising, curling in the air and clouding the partition between us.

Lenny turns over his shoulder, and even before he can sense who's standing here, watching him, you can tell he's jolted, real shaken even, on account of not expecting no one here, at this time. He screws up his eyes, so I bet he's looking for his own self, mirrored back to him—only to catch sight of me.

In a flash he spots my outline, like, through them spots on the murky glass.

Lenny gets up from the chair, awful stiff, and in one limp he comes to a stand right there, opposite me. My God, he looks strange today, and not only because he looks kinda naked, I mean, without them glasses. His gray hair isn't even combed, like he's awakened right this minute, after a fierce fight with a pillow or something—or else, he hasn't slept a wink last night, just like me.

Only in his case it happened who knows where.

Me, I look straight at him. His eyes, they have something wild in them: tender one second, mad the next, with wrinkled skin under them, sagging like squashed, hollow bags. He leans into the glass, laying his hands left and right of me, but I can't be sure what's in his head, like, if he wishes to plead with me, knowing I'm soon gonna forgive him—or else, he wishes to wring the life out of my throat.

But he don't try to do neither one nor the other. Instead he says, "Anita," kinda gruff, "where is my son? You must know where he is, don't you?"

And me, I shrug, 'cause like, what am I, his keeper?

So again Lenny comes, "Look, I've checked his bed. I know he did not sleep in it."

And I say, "So? Neither did you!"

His eyes flutter for a second, like he tries to ignore what I've just said, and how bitter it must feel to be dumped, even if it's only for a night.

So I say, "Ben isn't a baby, anyhow. And he didn't sleep in *my* bed, if that's what you're saying—even if you ain't saying it, exactly."

And he says, "Listen, dear—"

And I say, "Stop calling me that! This word, it sure as hell don't have no meaning to you."

He steps back, all the way back to his desk, as if slapped all of a sudden by a gust of cold wind. So at once—in spite of my anger—my heart goes out to him.

"I am dead serious," he says. "For the life of me I cannot find certain papers. The boy cannot have them, Anita. Not yet. Not while I am still alive. Where is he?"

And I say, "Last thing I know, me and him, we was like, playing the piano."

"From what I am told," says Lenny, "the two of you were banging like a pair of lunatics."

And me, I shrug, which in a flash, ignites the fury in him. I know Lenny: he can be terribly jealous. He claims that jealousy is like a compliment, almost; the most honest compliment a man can give. In his mind I should be happy, awful happy that he loves me so crazy, so deep.

But never did I see him like that: torn.

When it comes to his boy, Lenny is usually so steady. He's been longing for him for so many years. I wish I had a pa like that. And even if my husband has some secrets, and things he don't share, still, I'm sure that as a father, he has an awful big heart—but now that Ben is back home, a change has come over the old man. He can't make up his mind between trusting his son—or suspecting him for a rival.

Lenny comes forward—nearly going into a skid—and with full force he bangs the glass door, like he wants it to crack, to fall down in pieces, and to scatter all over the floor, with sharp shards ringing, pinging around me, 'cause like, he can see something in me, something invisible, that no one else can see: a mark, a see-through mark on my neck, like, from the touch of his son, zipping up my little black dress, a stain left there by accident, almost.

So he demands, "I need to talk to him. Now you tell me, where the hell is he?"

Which brings a little voice into my head, whispering something ma used to say, which is, "Charm the snake and then, real slow, back away."

So I say, real soft and gentle, "You know, Lenny, you have two sons—not one. Right now, I know where one of them is."

And I unbuckle my pink belt, and open my winter coat—just enough to let him see how my dress clings to my belly, which looks kinda puffy, 'cause it isn't exactly flat no more.

And from the inner pocket of my coat I bring out a picture, which I must admit is kinda confusing, 'cause at first glance it's like, nothing more than a mishmash of gray, so you can't exactly get it—not all at once, anyhow.

So you must learn to be awful patient, and take your time to study them lights and shadows here, in the picture, like, real slow and careful—or else, have someone else come to your help, and point out that, like, this is the inside of me, and this here, see, is a nose, and this, the lips of my sweet baby boy.

I bring the picture up and hold it for Lenny, pressing it right here, against the glass, just above the smudge, which his hand has just left there, on the other side.

I bet he can tell, by the glint in my eyes, that this here is like, real special, because looking at it you must also imagine the beat, the heartbeat going blip, blip, blip across the screen, from left to right, which means the baby is doing fine, real fine.

For a second Lenny is drawn to me, to the smile on my lips— but then, just before he can take a good look at the picture or say nothing, the phone rings.

So with a long screech he slides open the door, and passes me by on his way to the hall, in a rush to answer the thing.

"Hello," he says. "Aunt Hadassa!"

And after a long pause, which means she's going at him real good, he slumps against the wall, saying, "What? What did you say? Is there something wrong, I mean, at your end of the line? No, I am fine. Really, I am. Thank you for asking. What? My hearing? It is just as fine, aunt Hadassa. It is just... Just, I am a bit surprised. I cannot believe what you have just said."

Then he says, "Let me see now, do I remember correctly? You used to hate her, didn't you? My God, how you cursed, how you laid out all the reasons why I shouldn't, under any circumstances, have married the girl—even if she is pregnant! And after the wedding, you would not even return my calls. I got a whole week of silence—thank God—after which it was back to the same old thing: there was no stopping you on the phone, lamenting what you called, the *sorry event*. Why, just yesterday you gave me an earful—didn't you?"

"What?" he cries. "Can you repeat that, now? Anita, *she* deserves better?"

His lips tighten. "Hell," he says, this time under his breath, so I can't barely guess the words, "what is the matter with everybody today?"

And back to his usual voice he tells her, "Yes, I *am* listening, aunt Hadassa, of course I am. Yes, I know I should be careful, much more careful with her. Really, I promise. Yes, I realize she is still dizzy. Of course, I will do that—"

And to himself Lenny mutters, like, "Everyone is telling me, lately, just what she deserves. Some even care so much about the two of us as to say it behind my back. I mean, my own son..."

Now he bends down, as if aunt Hadassa is weighing him down, somehow.

"Well, fine," he tells her. "I will talk to him, too—but really, I can assure you—"

By now, his hand is well on its way to put the phone down, but then he jerks it up, just to say, "No. No, you are quite wrong. Really. I find him to be a well adjusted young man. Well, as happy as can be expected, of course, under the circumstances."

"No, I am not at all worried about him. And no," he gasps, "there is none of that. As far as I can tell. No. Absolutely nothing. No trace of jealousy."

And then, at last, the old man drops the thing in its cradle.

When he finally comes to bed that night, Lenny lays there for a long time without even stirring, as if he can't bring himself to close the gap, or even to try to reach over it, somehow, and touch me. I bet that in his head it's like, a ceasefire, and so me and him, we must build what so far, we've managed to destroy— by which he means, our defenses.

And so he figures that we can, perhaps, be safe from injury, and safe from inflicting it—but only if we hide from each other. I swear, this isn't no way to end a battle.

Lenny's kinda silent, except for heaving a sigh from time to time, which means he's still tied up at trying to hide feeling guilty—but anyhow, he isn't quite ready to forgive, or to be forgiven.

Then, out of the blue he says, not exactly to me but to the dark ceiling over us, "You know, I have thought about aunt Hadassa, what she said."

And me, I say, "Oh Lenny, just forget it," real soft.

And I roll away from my edge, a little closer to his side of the bed, like, half the distance to him, hoping he'll come halfway too and just, just hold me.

Instead, he's holding his grudge.

In a dry, guarded tone Lenny says, "I've left you an envelope on the kitchen table. First thing tomorrow morning I want you to take it, count the money, and then," he don't even say, *Anita,* "then go open a bank account in your name."

And I go, "What's that for, all of a sudden?"

And he goes, "Let it not be said that I am not giving you that which you deserve."

And in my aching heart I'm telling him, like, What I deserve is not to be made to feel like some fucking bitch. I'm your wife now. Before the wedding we used to have something, like, some good moments, some places where we was happy together. Can't you fight, Lenny, to get us back there?

Which is when he turns over, in a big hurry, to the other side, like there's something real exciting to be found over there. Then —before I have a chance to say nothing to him—his breathing gets awful deep, so I reckon he's fallen asleep.

Meanwhile, a distant rumble can be heard from outside.

It comes in fits, and from time to time reaches closer, rattling the window pane. I lay there wide awake, listening to the thunder, dreading what I know is sure to come next. I count the seconds in my head till finally, here it is: a fork of lightning comes tearing through in the night sky, zig zagging across the half-turned blinds.

And in a blinding flash my wedding dress, which is hung right there, opposite me, in the corner of the bedroom, comes alive. The heavy satin rustles like it's just about to breathe. The lace trembles in the cold air. And for a moment the beading glitters. It blinks, like it's trying to bring back some memory. So bright, so dazzling!

Then the dress sinks back into the dark.

So I slip off the bed, and feel my way, somehow, to the window to bolt it, and to turn them blinds, so Lenny won't wake up to the sound of the storm, 'cause clearly, you can tell that he needs his rest.

Now I touch something. It feels kinda round. Must be the oval frame, the frame of the standalone mirror, which used to belong to his ex-wife, Natasha.

I turn my head away, so as not to catch sight of the face—the pale, wide-eyed face, which I try to tell myself, is mine—but already, it's too late to believe that. Piercing me, out of the black void of the glass, is her sad, heart-rending look.

Which brings a thought into my head: Natasha, she isn't my enemy no more, because at this point it's over, I ain't a threat to her. Like, now I ain't the *other woman* no more.

Instead, I've grown to become what she used to be.

So it shouldn't scare me so, I mean, the fact that we look so much alike, because at last I've come full circle, just to learn—like she did, at the time—how bitter it feels, to see the moment coming, and be too weak to stop it, or even to avert your eyes, when you find yourself betrayed.

I can't change none of the things I've done to get here, and none of what it takes to be here, in her place—but I this I swear: never before did I feel this sorrow, this dark, crushing sorrow for what happened, and for how she ended up.

Like ma used to say, The only hope you have, Anita, is to look at yourself in the mirror—and find regret.

I cross to the window, which is the moment I begin hearing the sound. On the surface it seems to blend with the howling of the wind, and the scraping of bare branches across the edge of the roof—except it isn't coming from outside, and it's just a whimper at first.

Even so, it takes me by surprise, 'cause Lenny don't dream—or so he says. And for sure, he don't never talk in his sleep, 'cause no matter if it's day or night, his jaw is set firm, and them muscles, they're always tight around his lips, which looks funny with his eyes closed, but also a bit stern.

Anyhow you can see, just by looking, that at this moment he isn't hardly his usual self. So I rush to his side—but can't get nothing, not a word of what he mumbles, because now that he's in the grip of some fear, he don't barely make sense.

It takes my breath away to look at Lenny, 'cause he feels awful helpless, like a baby, almost. After a while he starts whining—not from his throat but from an inner place, deep down in his guts. From there he wails, wrapped up in his nightmare, as if he's about to be cut away, like, lose the one dear to him.

Me, I reckon it's something you might expect, like, when you're expecting: my heart pounds with great worry inside me, so much so that it hurts, even, like I'm already a mama—and not only to my little one.

So the fact that Lenny, he's like, twice my age, flies clear out of my head. I cuddle him, real gentle, and feel his big body trembling here, in my arms. And I rock him back and forth, back and forth, like he's a child, and I try to calm him down, whispering, "Sh... Sh..." And I hug him, even tighter now, 'cause he's shaking like a leaf. "What is it, Lenny?"

By now his voice is so intense. It's rising, rising to a shriek, "Taaah! Taaah—"

Which is when I figure, like, he's trying to call someone, call her back, real urgent, to make her stop just there—just before she reaches the rift, the edge of what he sees in his dream—so he don't end up losing her.

So I murmur, close to his ear, "Here I am... All's fine, I promise. I'm here, by your side, my dear, dear Lenny. Don't you worry."

And again he calls, only softer this time, "Taaah..."

I let his head lean on me, on my bare shoulder, and at once the chill's gone, both inside and out, because I kiss him—so long and so tender—right here, in the middle of his forehead. And I hope I can take on his burden, that burden of guilt, and of pain too, because in the end I don't really mind, I don't care no more if the name he's calling is mine—or else, if it is Natasha.

The Long Wait

Chapter 13

Then he says to his son, You should go, because this place can't hold the two of us for much longer, and because a young fellow like you must be hungry for adventure, and eager to see the world, and the last thing you want is to remain here, stuck in this stuffy place, with a grumpy old man, so here's some money, it should be more than enough—if spent modestly—for travel expenses, and stay in touch, and good luck with everything.

And Ben tries to say No, quite to the contrary, there's much more space now than there ever was, with the grand piano cleared out of the way, just look at Anita over there, stretching her arms and doing quick twirls, all across the room.

At hearing all that, Lenny just clenches his jaw—but he don't even grumble or nothing, and I bet he's holding his tongue just to drive home the point, like, how calm he manages to be, and how there isn't no sign of anger in him, or nothing.

All the same Ben seems to know that he's being punished. So without even glancing at me—like I'm the one to be blamed for all this—he bites his lip and goes into his room, where he can't help kicking the wall once or twice, after which he comes out to the kitchen, and kicks the refrigerator and then opens it, to look for an ice pack.

Then Ben spends some time wandering in and out of the living room, and making noise, long enough for his father to change his mind if he wanted to, or even to forgive him outright, for whatever it is that needs to be forgiven—but Lenny has already gone out to the balcony, where he can't hear nothing, not even me pleading with him, asking what happened, what the hell happened between them.

His silence is new to me. It's like, shouting from the walls. And what I read into it is like, if I didn't show so much leg back then, when he first laid eyes on me, ten years ago in that ice cream shoppe, and if I didn't wear them hot pink, high heel shoes, which forced him, somehow, to lose his head over me— which could never have happened otherwise—then things would be totally different now:

Nothing would end up tearing this family apart, and instead, the piano would still be crouching in place, and Natasha, his first wife, would still be here to play it—or at least, to pass her hand fondly over its back, and twiddle her fingers when she's done checking for dust, and smiling to herself, because like, all's well. All would be just fine.

Lenny acts like I'm some stray kitten that's wandered in here, and he's taking his distance. He isn't nowhere near me, and like, he's deaf to his son, on account of the noise, 'cause of punching them keys, the keys of his typewriter, pretty damn hard.

So at last Ben says to him, he says, "Fuck you, and your fucking money!" and turns to his room, and packs his stuff, like his old family Album, and that manila envelope with them bunches of hundred dollar bills, which I thrust, on impulse, into his hands, 'cause at that moment there's some immense force in my heart, which is stronger than me, and it makes me care for him awful deep, which is totally a surprise to me, and even more than that, a mistake.

It's against everything I've planned in my head, and I know it —but still, I don't even care at this point if Lenny happens to see it.

Then Ben buckles his rumpled suitcase. His long lashes cast a shade over his eyes, hiding how confused he must feel right now, and his slender body is strained, not so much because of the suitcase, but because of something that only the two of us can share: the burden of being young.

Then, without saying goodbye—not even to me—he's out the door.

In the first couples of months or so after his son left, Lenny's been very quiet. In some ways, things ain't all that bad between us. He comes home every night, even asks—when he cares to look at me—if the baby's started kicking already. His question is kinda polite, and it don't really break the silence, just marks a place from where we can restart it.

Anyhow we're together, so I don't have to worry no more about where he is, and I don't have to call aunt Hadassa, who has her sources, and I don't have to listen to her squirming, trying to spare me from knowing what this entire town already knows, which is, that Lenny's been sleeping around.

It's always the same thing now. Me and him sit down at the kitchen table and eat dinner together, like a normal family, except that we do it in silence. Then we settle into that old, sagging couch—him in one corner, me in the other—and wait. What it is we're waiting for isn't exactly clear. At first I could swear it was, like, a word from Ben—but now I figure it's a good thing the day's getting shorter.

Tonight—the first moonless night of this winter—I can sense a change in Lenny, which starts, for me, with the scent of his aftershave.

It's Aqua Velva. It's been a long time since I've caught it on him, and I can get a bit tipsy just by tipping over, like, to take it in. He grips the faded armrest and gets up, with some effort, from his corner, and puts on his fingerless leather gloves, with which he can type, especially on cold nights. Then he goes out to the balcony, and I can see him fumbling for something there, in the drawers of his desk. Finally he brings back a handful of tapes—I hope none of them is mine—and the tape recorder, which he sets up across from me, on the floor next to Beethoven's bust.

From down there Lenny turns to me, and I see the question in his eyes, like, Is it too late already, for the two of us?

And aloud he says, "Anita? Want to dance?"

Over the last couple of months he hasn't given voice to no anger, and neither have I, which I figure can't hardly be bad, 'cause without words any feeling—even rage—can peter out, so that one of these days, it's gonna be left there, dull and limp, somewhere behind us. It can happen, 'cause his son isn't here between us, and time passes.

Like ma used to say, Time heals all wounds. Which sounds pretty stale, but it must be true, 'cause I've stopped thinking by now about my youth going to waste. Instead I'm thinking about the fact that I've stopped thinking about that.

So in the end, we're back where we started, almost. Lenny's my man. He's mine. Me, I'm his. All's clear. Nothing gets confused.

"Well?" he murmurs. "Do you?"

I reckon the reason he's talking to me, like, under his breath, isn't only because he's unsure of me, of what I'll say after the long, icy silence—but also because he can't stand the echo, which seems to have moved in here with us lately.

So I whisper, as soft as I can, "I do."

He inserts one of them tapes, and sets the tape recorder to *Rewind*, then *Play*. At first I almost expect *my* voice to come on, but then, by the spring in his step as he's coming over, I figure it's gonna be music. He reaches out to me, so I peel off his glove, and his touch feels nice, it's warm and strong, the way I remember it.

Lenny helps me out of the sofa, which is good, 'cause I feel pretty heavy lately, and if I stand up by myself I tend to stop, just to look down to check if I my feet can still be spotted there, under the round mound of my belly.

I rise into his arms, and note that his forehead comes down more heavily than ever, right over his eyebrows, and the crease in the middle—which as always, remind me of my pa—is deeper now. He must have shrunk a little, too. Maybe not, maybe it's just something I imagine.

Now Lenny lays his hands on my hips, careful at first, like we're strangers. If we was strangers for real, things would get wilder, faster. I draw a bit closer, and put my hand on his shoulder, and rise to the tips of my toes to reach up, to comb his thinning hair, awful gentle, with my fingers. I slick it back, 'cause in my eyes it's always made him look so handsome, like one of them old movie stars.

In turn, his hand brushes my hair, gathering it up, for a second, into a pony tail, and I close my eyelids, feeling how at first he hesitates. The old man waits there for a long while, before leaning over and kissing them.

I bet that like me, he remembers that night, the first time we danced, 'cause now that the tape recorder has finished giving out the long, rustling hush, and the music comes on, it's the old song, doubled by a ghost of its sound: something slow from the sixties, which years ago used to bring tears to ma's eyes, 'cause like, it awakened her to being lonely, and now it brings them to mine.

Lenny cups my face in his hand and pecks me lightly on the cheek. Then he starts showering me with the littlest kisses, all along the trail of tears, his mouth slipping down the skin of my neck. And I laugh—not only on account of being ticklish, but because suddenly I'm aroused, and even a touch nervous. And I say, "Let's just dance," which is echoed, like, by the laughter of the walls.

So Lenny backs away and I come, and then in reverse, he comes as I back away, and we go and come, come and go this way for a long while—but we don't hardly move from the same spot, here by the sofa, even though there's so much space now around us, for dancing and what not.

It's not only me wondering about it—it's Beethoven as well, his blank eyes following every one of our moves from down there, on the floor, like he's annoyed at his bad luck, having to witness all this—and in slow motion, too!—and his neck, despite being solid, must be terribly cramped, and like, he hopes to be relieved of that pain pretty soon, and stretch his neck, and could we please stop idling there like some tired old couple, and come stomping off in his direction, and break it already.

By now Lenny has undone the buttons of my blouse, and he loosens it this way and that, and then, in one firm pull it's already down, which allows him to take one breast in his mouth, and lick the skin all around it.

At once, my nipple grows big. He gives it up in favor of the other one, which he starts sucking. Now I'm divided between my two halves, 'cause the first breast, which is wet, starts cooling off as it dries, and the second is like, burning. I twist my body side to side, to offer him first the one, then the other, and again.

Pretty soon we go out of order, and in a heated haste we find ourselves tossing the pillows of the sofa to the floor, first the pillow out of what is usually his corner, then the one out of mine, and we stumble rolling down, till we land on top of them, more or less. So he cocks his head, looking up at me, waiting, 'cause like, now it's me on top. And it's at that second, just as I start groping for the zipper of his crutch, that—out of the blue —the doorbell rings.

But like, there's nobody there.

By the time Lenny returns from the door, I've crossed the floor on all four, all the way to Beethoven, and turned him around so he don't face us no more, and instead he points his nose at the corner, and I've come right back to lay, in a foxy pose, on them pillows.

But somehow, I know that Lenny knows that we ain't exactly in the mood no more.

"Who—who was that?" I ask.

And he says, "No one."

And I point at what he carries behind him, in his hand, "And what's this?"

And shrugging, he says, "Don't know."

And I say, "So, open it."

And real stubborn, he says, "Don't want to."

So half nude I rush to the kitchen, and bring a kitchen knife and cut through the flap of the box, and there—to my surprise —lays a bottle of Rosé Champagne, flanked by two stemmed glasses, the kind you can stack in layers to build them champagne towers, like the one we had at our wedding.

At first, my bet is that this is a gift from my husband—who else—which takes my breath away, it's so cool, so awesome, especially because I haven't gotten nothing from him lately.

So I twist my hips walking up to him, and snatch one of them glasses and put it in place, right over my left breast. Before I got pregnant, and become so full of curves, it would have been a perfect fit—but now, not so much.

Then, just before opening my mouth to ask him to uncork the bottle, I realize my mistake.

"Take it off, take that thing off right now, right this minute," he stammers, and his forehead curves down over him even heavier and more wrinkled than before. I can't even blame him, or no one, 'cause really, I reckon it's too late for us.

So without saying a word I obey him, and remove the glass from my heart, and watch him, again in silence, as he rummages through the box in search of a note, or something. Which he finds, finally, down there at the bottom. In square, printed letters the note reads simply, "To Anita."

No return address, no signature, no date, nothing.

The old man looks long and hard into my eyes, like he's searching for answers, not exactly sure if to punish me, like I was a naughty school girl, or to send me back home to my ma. After a while he figures he can't do neither, so he just turns his back on me, and punches the box so it can collapse on itself, and stuffs it in the garbage can, along with the uncorked bottle and them two glasses. Then he goes to the bathroom, and the water starts running for his shower.

I try not to be angry, or hurt. I sit there in the dark, and wait. I can't tell exactly what it is I'm waiting for.

So, *Rewind. Record.*

What is there to say? I reckon it's stupid, it don't make no sense to hunger so bad for a change. Still... It's a strange feeling, knowing that someone out there is playing with a thought about me, daring me to risk everything I've got, like, this marriage, this shelter for my baby and me—all for nothing. For a bottle of champagne.

The water's still running in the shower, wisps of vapor escaping as far as here in the living room. By now the glass door is all steamed out, so the balcony out there, which is facing ours, is pretty much washed out, and you can't see the wintery sky no more, and you can't even tell that it's moonless. And like, everything is suddenly nothing but a guess—except for one thing:

I swear, I must be crazy. I know I am, 'cause the only path to see clear out of this place is through what I write here, into the steam, on the cold, hard surface, with my finger.

Ben.

Around Me Around Him

Chapter 14

A unt Hadassa calls me to say that he's called her, this time from New York, just to say hi and to let her know all's well, he's traveling around the country, having the time of his life. So I tell her, like, Good for him, and I mean it—but I'm careful not to mention no doubts, 'cause like, why should I make her worry. So the only one I ask is myself, Why do I still have that funny feeling, like he's never left town?

Like, a week ago I went shopping with her, and we stopped on Montana street, outside the window of a baby furniture store, 'cause that cradle—the one with the arched canopy, with them cute ruffles over it—caught my eye, it was so adorable! And then, then I could swear I spotted them eyes glinting there, in the glass. That look, it was terribly familiar. So without having to turn around I already knew that someone, someone I used to know was standing there, directly behind us, on the other side of the street.

I won't have noticed that man at all, if not for the odd way the chin was wrapped with a scarf, over the nose and ears, which wasn't even necessary, 'cause there wasn't no wind, and it was such a warm, sunny March day.

But it turned out that it wasn't Ben, after all. I mean, the shoes wasn't exactly right, and way he walked away was kinda different. And the hair was all wrong, it was much too long. And, he wasn't even looking at me, the way I thought he was. Like, there wasn't even a glance. I really don't get it. I thought I had a sharp eye, but somehow I must have misread the reflection.

Enough, I told myself then, what's the matter with you?

You think someone—anyone—would bother taking another look at you now, waddling around with your belly coming forward like that, like a beach ball?

Then we went into the store, aunt Hadassa and me, and I think she could tell—in spite of me trying to smile—how tense I was. So she bought a little something for me—well, for the baby, really: a mobile, with plush toy animals dancing around it. For now, I mean, until I get a cradle for my baby, it's hung up in the bedroom window, right in the center, where the blinds meet.

So at night, when I feel sad, or tired, or just sleepy, I pull out the little string to wind the thing up, which makes the animals go fly—fly like a dream—so slowly around your head.

And at the same time, it brings out a sweet lullaby, chiming, *Twinkle, twinkle, little star... How I wonder what you are...*

I stand here, by the window under the mobile. I touch the glass between one blind and another, and watch them animals, mirrored. They come in like ghosts, one after another, right up to the surface, swing around, and fly back out, into the dark. Then I gaze at them stars up there, so far beyond, and ask myself if they're real—or am I, again, misreading some reflection.

But after a while, all of that don't matter no more.

What matters is only what's here. I touch my skin right under my breasts, which is where the little one's curled, and where he kicks, 'cause he has to. Like, he don't feel so cosy no more. Here, can you feel it? I reckon he wants me to talk to him. He can hear me inside, for sure. He can hear every note of this silvery music.

It ripples all around him, wave after wave. I can tell that it's starting to sooth him. It's so full of joy, of delight, even if to him, it's coming across somewhat muffled. Like a dream in a dream, it's floating inside, into his soft, tender ear.

I close my eyes and hold myself, wrapping my arms real soft—around me around him—and I rock ever so gently, back and forth, back and forth, with every note of this silvery marvel. You can barely hear me—but here I am, singing along. I'm whispering words into myself, into him.

And this is the moment when, like one, we're happy.

Not The End

Chapter 15

He's been so busy, punching away at the machine and crumpling page after page into the trash bin, that lately I can't get a word through to him no more. Oh, he's replacing this tape with another and like, listening to my voice all the time—but not to me.

Which makes me wish sometimes that I was some written piece, some character in his book, 'cause I would be more real to him that way. I see myself as *her*, a thing of fiction springing to life, like, right out of them letters—which are so dense, so crammed on that sheet of paper, that there isn't no space to breathe—and smoothing all them creases in me with a slight, crispy rustle, which for sure, would win his attention right away.

I bet he would let himself stretch the truth about me to create her, 'cause like, the paper can take it. His story would draw the longest legs and the sexiest ass and the most perfect pair of boobs you could ever dream up. What's more, she would become a mouth, like, for things that go on in his head, things so fucking raw and intense that they frighten him.

Them words he writes, they would all come out of her lips, stained with ink and scratched out here and there, to say the things that in real life Lenny wishes he could blurt out, yet holds himself back, as best he can, from doing so. But then, that Anita won't be *me*.

By now I've learned my lesson, I learned it good: I won't leave no more pieces of me laying around. When I'm done with the tape recorder I pop my tape out, and stash it away at once, like, behind Beethoven's bust or under it or some other such place, and I cover it with papers and stuff.

This way Lenny don't get it in his hands, to listen to my voice, to study the way I *enunciate* things, so he don't have no excuse to ignore the *real* me. And what's more, he can't get hurt by what he don't hear, by what wasn't meant for his ears in the first place, so he don't feel so jealous no more, and like, he don't try to forget it, to blank out how hurt he is.

Which is good, 'cause then there isn't no need to argue between us, like, if he's the one betraying my trust by listening to my tape—or I'm the one betraying his, by what I say.

Anyhow, this evening he's different. I hear him pacing around the balcony, between his desk and the wall behind his chair, which is a small feat all by itself, 'cause like, there isn't barely room to move out there. Then, after two hours of this Lenny throws his hands in the air, and comes in to tell me he's stuck.

Which makes me raise one of my eyebrows, like, "You sure don't look stuck to me, 'cause here you are, running around." And what I mean by *running around* is clear to both of us.

What can he say to that? Nothing, that's what.

Anyhow, I don't want to sound bitter at him, 'cause I care for Lenny, really, I do. So I ask, "Now, how d'you mean, stuck?"

And he says, "Oh, stop it. You are never going to understand me."

And I say, "Just try me, Lenny."

And he goes, "I am stuck, stuck, stuck! Stuck in a rut! I will never succeed in getting anything done. I am wasting time here, exhausted, not being able to think, and why? Because unwittingly, I am too busy complaining to myself over my wasted time."

And before I can tell him to stop talking nonsense, or else put it in writing, he goes on to say, "Damn it. I cannot write a single line."

"But like, why?"

"Because," he groans, "every word gets me closer to *The End*."

So I try this, I say, "Maybe there is no end, really, and all you can do is just cut off at any point, because life just goes on, like, even if you leave me right here, right in the middle of a sentence. That," I say, "could be *The End*, too."

"No, no, no! It is not that simple."

"I bet it's simpler than you think."

"No," he says, "I am not *that* tired, not yet. Cannot abandon it, cannot leave off just like that, in the middle, because the story needs something, it needs to be completed—but then, I do not know where it goes from here, and for the life of me, I cannot find *The End*, even though I know—I know it's closing in on me."

"If you can't add no words, don't you think you're already done?"

"No," he says. "At this point, no. I cannot stop writing—and I cannot write. I am left in midair, hanging from a cliff."

"So? Just let go."

And he stares at me strange, "Wouldn't you like that."

I ain't exactly sure I get what he means by that, but instead of explaining Lenny runs back to the balcony and leans over his desk, scribbling something real fast in the margin of a page, like he is chasing some idea with his pen. Then he waves his hand, pretty wild, calling me to come out there and listen.

He pushes his bifocals up his nose, which is totally useless, 'cause they just slip down again. And this is what he reads to me:

She knew not to expect hearing the end of the sentence, because the old man had already slammed the door behind him. She could guess where Leonard was heading, probably to that fake old blond, who lived on the southern fringe of town.

The next morning she woke up to the sound, the insistent sound of knocks at the door, and a sudden fear squeezed her heart as she opened it, to find two grim-faced cops.

When they hesitated to say what they came in to say, she screamed. She did not want to learn that the old man had been found lifeless, nor did she want to see the snapshots they had taken, right there at the scene, snapshots that revealed all the tedious details of how he had ended up lying there, with a half crooked smile, in the other woman's arms.

"Awesome!" I tell Lenny. "I'm so glad to hear this."

His eyes pop, "You are?"

"Sure!" I say. "Me, I was kinda afraid you're writing something real, like, something about us. Now—with what you've come up with, right there—I can see awful clear that it ain't nothing but fiction."

By way of an answer Lenny crumples the page, and sinks back in his chair, muttering something about how I don't understand him, him and his creative ideas and this particular blueprint he is drafting, for a new kind of a novel, and what a damn fool he is, like, every time he repeats the mistake of using me for a listener.

"Then," I say, "find yourself someone else to listen. Me, I don't much like the sound of how you wrote it."

"The sound?" his eyes widen once more. "What sound? And, what is wrong with it?"

"Noise," I say. "Just too much of it! That's what you get when you try to end things, like, with a bang. Me, I don't even want to imagine all that slamming, and them knocks at the door and what not. Come here, I want you to hear something."

I take him by the hand, and somehow Lenny lets me. He's curious, I bet, so I lead him straight to the bedroom. I come to a stop right there, under the musical mobile, which I hung just last night in the window, between one blind and another.

Then, I pull the little string, so the thing starts turning around, and playing its tender notes. "There... Hear this? Now here's a sound I do like."

He closes his eyes to listen, so I ain't exactly sure what he sees in his head. After a while Lenny says, "You know, I like it too. Just a delicate little whisper of a lullaby. Maybe you are right, Anita. Maybe that is what I need. Maybe that is what is called for, I mean, not just to heal both of us—but also, to complete the story. Listen! Here is a note—I could just detect it, just now —a note that could mark the end."

"But then," I say, "it could mark a beginning, just as well."

And for the first time this evening he looks straight into my eyes. At that moment I can tell that he sees me, like, for what I am. I mean, he sees beyond what he's put on paper, with them longest legs and that sexiest ass and them boobs and what not. Yes, now he sees in me something more than all that, something else: a woman, expecting.

At that instant a sudden pain makes itself known in me, right down my back. It starts turning there, deep in my belly. Which is when I figure that I've felt it before. It's come and gone several times this evening—only it seemed awful dull up to now, which like, lets me ignore it.

This time it's sharper, and it lasts quite a while, which makes me wince. "Aw," I say.

But anyhow, Lenny don't even hear me, 'cause he's back to scratching his head, on account of being confused about his story, and about what this music could tell you, and how he could use it in his story, like, to mark the end.

"Yes," he whispers. "Just a sound of bells, chiming, chiming, chiming. And behind that, the breath of a baby asleep in the cradle, rocked to sleep by a mother's hand. Maybe that is what is needed."

"Aw," I say again.

And he says, "Such a gentle sound. No doubt, Ben would like it."

I stare at him in surprise, 'cause for several months Lenny's been so mad, so angry at his son, that he didn't hardly mention his name—nor did he allow me to mention it.

"So now," I say, like, with caution, "all's fine? Like, you've forgiven him?"

"I do not know about that," he says, sounding pretty touchy.

A minute later his voice seems to soften. "What I *do* know—I can feel it in my bones—is this: any day now, my son will be coming here, to my door, and—"

"You have two sons, not one," I cut in.

"He will be coming back," says Lenny, right over my words. "Looking for the thing, the one thing only I can give him: a story."

Me, I can tell he don't pay no attention to anything I say, so all I can do is at this point is just breathe hard for a few seconds, and then repeat, "Aw," a third time.

Meanwhile Lenny's busy arguing with himself.

"Whenever I read what I've written, it seems so sketchy to me, so goddam fragmented! Just a jumble of moments, and some voices here and there, lost in the clutter. What am I missing? How come I find myself falling short, so terribly short of where I thought I was going? What the story needs is a meaning—or else all my work, and all my sleepless nights have come to nothing, nothing, nothing in the end."

His eyes seem to beg me for some hint, some meaning, like I could give it to him. What can I say to that? Nothing, and he knows it.

So Lenny starts pacing around the bed, and he reaches the mirror, the oval mirror standing there, slightly tilted, in the corner. Here he stops, and glances at the scribbled page over there, in his reflected hand.

From where I stand, them letters look pretty odd, them words scrambled—right turned left, in turned out—right there, on that patch of white, clutched by the ghost of his hand, deep in the glass. Lenny leans in, so his nose nearly touches that other nose, the one in the mirror, like he's trying to go in, to read what's in there. And his shadow inside, it's trying to read, just as hard, what's out here.

It's like, a riddle, waiting to be solved.

His bifocals, they've come loose from his face and dropped off, so he searches for them here and there across the floor. No matter, he'll find them later. Then, like, by mistake, Lenny gets too close to the mirror and—bang!—hits his forehead against it. I ain't exactly sure how it's happened. Anyhow, you can tell he's growing restless, 'cause the paper in his hand starts rustling, till the writing becomes just a blur, on both sides of the glass.

"There must be *some* significance to all this," he mutters. "And it must be extracted. It must be put in words—or else, my son would open the door, and I—I would not be ready for him."

"So?" I say. "What is it you're afraid of?"

"Ben would come in, and there would be no one to see but an old man, an old man standing there, his mouth open as if to start singing, and just cold breath coming out."

And with that Lenny pushes the frame of the mirror, so now it's tilted awful sharp, and it's like, sticking clear out of the corner, right here between me and him. He lifts a hand, like, to correct it, to straighten the thing, which is when we start hearing the knocks.

Them knocks, they come rapping, rapping real timid at first, there at the entrance door. Then comes a squeal, like that of a key which—having been inserted—starts turning, real slow, in the lock.

The old man turns his back to the mirror, which is still pretty crooked.

"My God," he mumbles. "Not now! I am not ready for him."

And then, then he takes a shaky step back, stumbling—

Play. Stop. Eject

Chapter 16

Next morning, I'm sent home empty-handed, while my baby must stay at the hospital a few more days, to get something called colored light therapy, 'cause like, he's been diagnosed with jaundice. But does anyone care? Hello there? I try to call home, for Lenny to come pick me up—but as usual I end up just managing, somehow, to get back on my own.

I open the bedroom window, and feel warm spring air coming in, blowing gently into my face, which feels like a promise. Like, it's gonna be good. It's gonna be a beautiful day.

I rewind the musical mobile, and listen to it chiming, chiming, chiming over my head for a long while. And there I stand listening, not knowing what to do, not wanting to admit to myself how I feel. Anyhow I'm glad you can't see me sniffling, and blotting the corner of my eye, 'cause like, there isn't no one here I can hug, and no one to hug me right back.

Lenny isn't back yet, and neither is Ben. The place seems kinda empty to me—more so than usual—like a spirit has left it, on account of the piano, which is gone, and the shattered mirror. And it's messy, because of the glass, which is strewn all around me, crushing underfoot as I move around the floor, until finally I stomp off to the corridor.

Then I'm empty. Exhausted. Can't bring myself to hold a broom straight, like, to sweep away all them broken pieces. In a daze I wander into Ben's bedroom, and within moments I'm asleep in his bed.

When I open my eyes again, it's already the next morning.

I wake up to a sound, an annoying sound of knocks at the door, and a sudden fear squeezes my heart as I open it, to find two grim-faced cops. It almost feels like I've read this story before.

When they hesitate to say, like, what they've come in to say, I make up my mind I ain't gonna scream. Instead I stick my thumbs in my ears, 'cause I don't want to hear, don't want to learn that my husband's been found lifeless. And for sure I don't want to be asked no questions, 'cause like, I don't hardly have answers.

I cup the palms of my hands over my eyes, 'cause I don't want to see the snapshots they're trying to show me, which was taken right there at the scene, snapshots that show him lying there, curled, in Natasha's arms. How he got there, no one seems to know—not even them cops. They want *me* to tell them, like, how it happened.

So in spite of myself I can't help peeking, between one finger and another, only to find that in some of them pictures, his face muscles seem awful relaxed. I bet it's just a trick of the camera, some flash, which makes him look like he's laughing, almost— even though the crease on his forehead hasn't barely smoothed up.

Which reminds me of my pa, who left me such a long time ago, that I can't remember nothing of his face no more, I mean, nothing but a crease just like this, in the middle of his forehead.

And even that's turning into a blur now. I swear, it's because of them tears. Damn, I miss him. I miss him so.

No, Lenny. I ain't gonna cry.

A week after the funeral, which I couldn't attend because of a sudden fever, I get a call from Lenny's attorney, Mr. Bliss. Which is a sure sign—if you didn't know it already—that this is a time of misery.

He coughs up something like, "Mrs. Kaminsky, I hope you shall know no more sorrow." And I go, "Really? That makes two of us."

Then Mr. Bliss goes on to say he's stunned, simply stunned to hear what's happened, and congratulations are in order, Mazel Tov for the baby, what's his name? And he can't find Ben, do I happen to know his address? A phone number, at least? No? And to come to his office just as soon as I can, because of the will, which Lenny has changed again only three days before his passing, and because of a key to some secret drawer in his desk, both of which must be handed over to me.

I don't exactly bother to tell him that I've known about that drawer for quite some time now, and that I've managed to pry it open—right after them cops finally left—with a kitchen knife.

It's like, I had to stab something, someone. If Lenny was gonna pop in right then, I was gonna kill him right on the spot.

What I found in the drawer was like, confusing. There was no way for me to read the whole thing clear through to the end, 'cause it was way too long, and anyhow, from the beginning, them letters was too small, and the writing too dense or something, which made me start yawning right away.

Even so, I know one thing: for Lenny, this must have been a labor of love, something he did for his son, for Ben to remember him by. I must find him, and let him know that.

Several times over the last few months, Ben would come in here—but only when I wasn't home. Like, he was invisible. He hated this place, but couldn't do without it. Them memories in his head, they would play tricks on him, pulling him back here. Also, I figure he wanted to stay close to his father. And to me too, I bet.

I could always tell, later, that I'd just missed him, because there was a trace of his smell, like, still hanging in the air, and because he'd moved things around: a pillow had been squeezed into the corner of his bed, or there was a new footprint in the dust. I swear, he must have wanted to be found out.

But not anymore—or else he'd be here, to talk to them cops. So I find myself saying what needs to be said—not directly to him, but to the tape recorder. I'm careful to sound as dry and cool as my voice would let me, 'cause you don't never know who's out there, listening.

When I'm done, I place the tape in its plastic case, and tuck it down there, behind Beethoven's bust, which I turn around to face the balcony, so the tip of its nose kinda shines in the daylight, which can draw your attention. I hope that sooner or later, Ben's gonna notice it. My voice sounds pretty formal—but it's too much, now, to do it over.

Your father left you a stack of pages here, in a secret drawer in his desk. It's his story, which he finished—or at least, was close to finishing it. I bet he wanted you to read the thing.

Where shall I mail it to? Let me know.

For two days I wait, and there isn't no answer.

Then, on the third day, I come in from my daily visit to my baby at the hospital, and the moment I unlock the door, I see that Beethoven has turned around, somehow, so its face is totally in the shade, but like, them marble eyes seem to glare pretty hard—this time at the entrance, at me. Tucked behind it, I spot the same tape I've used—except it isn't in the plastic case no more.

So my heart starts to hammer, inside. I put the tape in the tape recorder, and *Play*. My voice isn't there. It's been erased. Overwritten. His voice sounds drier, and even cooler than mine. It says:

Burn it.

Which sets me back on my heels. At once, I go ahead to *Record*:

It don't belong to me. You do it.

This time, a whole week passes by until Beethoven swings around. Ben's voice says:

I can't. This story has our voices in it.

So I say:

I bet he tried to write 'us'—but them characters ain't who we are. Now, the thing I'm worried about is not his story—but the tapes, which I'm about to destroy. Unless you tell me not to.

It's just, I don't want them to be found, 'cause the cops were here twice already. It's like, they ain't exactly sure what to look for. They don't seem to get how Lenny hit his head on the mirror and still managed to get to Sunrise home, with no one seeing him coming in. They don't really believe that's what happened.

I bet they suspect I might have killed him—but like, why would I stash his body in someone's bed, let alone Natasha's? Then, there's Mr. Bliss: he tells me now he wants to visit, to give me his condolences or something.

So by tomorrow, our voices is like, history. Gonna be erased. Or, if you wish to keep them, I can mail them tapes to you. Just tell me where to.

A week drags by—seven sleepless nights—during which I find myself missing my ma so much that it hurts, because now that the little one is finally here, I don't even get how she did it, like, how she managed to take care of me all these years, all on her own. No wonder she ended up being grumpy, which is one thing I'd rather forget.

Between feedings I go through the process, erasing one tape after another. I do it by recording stuff over them. What kind of stuff? Just anything.

Like, my baby crying at night. The way his whining turns into a giggle as I touch my nipple to his lips, just before he settles into his rhythm, like, suck, suck, swallow, breathe; suck, suck, swallow, breathe. The way I lay him over my shoulder and pat his back, to ease the hiccups. The distant sound of a door sliding along its track, as the neighbor comes out to her balcony—the one opposite us—to water her pot of geraniums. Some kid out there, practicing his piano. Stuff.

Then, late one evening, I notice the tape's changed place. This time, it's out in the open, right under Beethoven's nose. It's like, a hint that there isn't no need to hide what we say to each other.

Ben's voice says:

I happened to be out of town for a few days, so did not get your warning in time, about the tapes I mean, nor could I stop you.

As to my father's story, I still do not know what to do with it. I glanced at it, lying there in that secret drawer, and even read a few passages, some of which were too painful for me—and others which I cared nothing for, as they seemed overly fictional.

At one point the whole stack fell out of my hands, and the papers spread out. I picked them up and stuffed them back in the drawer, as best I could—but they are totally scrambled now. I doubt I can rearrange them so they will be in the right order, I mean, his order, the way he wrote it. Can you?

I wish I had the tapes, but what's gone is gone.

I say to myself, Oh shoot, and let a week go by before responding:

I did give you time to stop me.

Ben's silent, no sign from him for more than a week. I ain't even sure if the tape's been touched, like, if he's got my message. I don't want to wait no more, so this morning, before going out for my walk down to Santa Monica beach, which I do every day with my baby, I record over my previous message:

Where are you? Me, I know you can't be too far.
You angry with me?

Later, like, twenty minutes into my walk, I figure I need a sweater for me, and a blanket or something for the little one, 'cause I reckon it's turning kinda windy. So I go back, and I think I see someone, some passerby running the other way, into the back alley.

I climb up the stairs, turning over my shoulder once or twice, to see if I can tell who it is, 'cause like, something about him looks awful familiar. But like, he's already gone.

Then, as the door opens, I see that the tape recorder's been moved, and I tell myself, Look! It's still recording! So I hurry in, *Stop, Rewind, Play,* and then I close my eyes, and like, I take him in, because I so enjoy the sound, the deep sound of his voice.

No, not angry.
How can I be? I will never forget what you did for me.
And later, I could not believe it when you pushed the yellow manila envelope into my hands, with all that money in it, the day dad threw me out. I only used a small portion of it, that first week. By now I've nearly replenished what was spent. I am working now, and plan to give you back the amount in full.
Oh, and another thing.

I'm so glad that in addition to that envelope, you put the photo album in my suitcase. I barely noticed when you did it, nor did I realize what it was that I carried out with me, as I left this place.

Since then, I cannot tell you, Anita, how many times I have taken the album out, and opened it to that one page, on which a picture used to be missing.

You must have noticed it: at the top, there is a picture of my mom, from the time she was very young—perhaps your age—and pregnant. At the bottom, there is a picture of a little boy fascinated by that single candle in front of him, on his birthday cake. In between these two pictures, there used to be another one, which—try as I may—I cannot remember. Strangely, it has gone missing.

In its place I find, to my surprise, a small, black-and-white ultrasound image. It shows a profile of a baby, curled in the womb. I know, of course, that it could not have been me. The photo paper is much too fresh, and hasn't even begun to yellow. Even so, that picture —which you must have inserted there—has filled a hole.

Somehow it makes me feel as if the first stages of my life have been fully recorded.

What can I say to that, except:

Don't look back, Ben.
Like, don't Rewind.
Play.

To which he answers, later that night:

Stop.

It is your turn now to find me.

Eject.

~ The End ~

To be continued with:

The "White
Piano

STILL LIFE WITH MEMORIES
VOLUME II

Or:

Apart
from Love

STILL LIFE WITH MEMORIES
VOLUME I AND II, WOVEN TOGETHER

About the Story

Falling in love with Lenny should have been the end to all her troubles. For Anita, it's only the beginning, when family secrets start unravelling. His ex-wife, Natasha, is succumbing to a mysterious disease. How can Anita compete with her shadow? How can she find a voice of her own?

And when his estranged son, Ben, comes back and lives in the same small apartment, can she keep the balance between the two men, whose desire for her is marred by guilt and blame?

Dealing with the challenging prospects of the marriage of opposites, this book can be read as a standalone novel as well as part of one of family sagas best sellers. Still Life with Memories is a family saga series tinged with family saga romance, fraught with marital issues, and riddled with the difficulty of connecting fathers and sons.

About the Author

U vi Poznansky is a *USA TODAY* bestselling, award-winning author, poet and artist. "I paint with my pen," she says, "and write with my paintbrush."

Uvi earned her B. A. in Architecture and Town Planning from the Technion in Haifa, Israel. During her studies and in the years immediately following her graduation, she practiced with an innovative Architectural firm, taking part in the design of a large-scale project, *Home for the Soldier*.

Having moved to Troy, N.Y. with her husband and two children, Uvi received a Fellowship grant and a Teaching Assistantship from the Architecture department at Rensselaer Polytechnic Institute. There, she guided teams in a variety of design projects and earned her M.A. in Architecture. Then, taking a sharp turn in her education, she earned her M.S. degree in Computer Science from the University of Michigan.

During the years she spent in advancing her career—first as an architect, and later as a software engineer, software team leader, software manager and a software consultant (with an emphasis on user interface for medical instruments devices)— she wrote and painted constantly. In addition, she taught art appreciation classes.

Her versatile body of work can be seen in two websites: her blog includes thoughts about the creative process, reader reviews, author interviews, excerpts from her novels, voice clips from her audiobooks, poems and short stories. Her <u>art site</u> includes bronze and ceramic sculptures, paper engineering projects, oil and watercolor paintings, charcoal, pen and pencil drawings, and mixed media.

Coma Confidential, Overkill, Overdose, and Overdue are novels in the *Ash Suspense Thrillers with a Dash of Romance* series. With each new case, Ash uses grit and intuition to solve the crime.

Virtually Lace is the first volume in a multi-author thriller series, *High-Tech Crime Solvers*, where the authors bring each other's characters into their books.

My Own Voice, The White Piano, The Music of Us, Dancing with Air, and *Marriage before Death* are novels in the *Still Life with Memories* series, a family saga with a love story that develops in the face of hardship and illness over two generations, starting at the 1980's, then harkening back to WWII when Lenny, a soldier, and Natasha, a rising star, first met. These books are also offered in two bundles: *Apart from Love* and *Apart from War*.

Rise to Power, A Peek at Bathsheba, and *The Edge of Revolt* are novels in *The David Chronicles*, telling the story of David as you have never heard it before: from the king himself, telling the unofficial version, the one he never allowed his court scribes to recount. In his mind, history is written to praise the victorious— but at the last stretch of his illustrious life, he feels an irresistible urge to tell the truth. These books are also offered in a trilogy.

In addition, *The David Chronicles* includes six art collections: *Inspired by Art: Fighting Goliath, Inspired by Art: Fall of a Giant, Inspired by Art: Rise to Power, Inspired by Art: A Peek at Bathsheba, Inspired by Art: The Edge of Revolt,* and *Inspired by Art: The Last Concubine.*

A Favorite Son, a new-age twist on an old yarn, is inspired by the biblical story of Jacob and his mother Rebecca, plotting together against the elderly father Isaac, who is lying on his deathbed.

Twisted is a unique collection, laden with shades of mystery. Here, you will come into a dark, strange world, a hyper-reality where nearly everything is firmly rooted in the familiar—except for some quirky detail that twists the yarn.

Home and *Can We Still Love*, Uvi's deeply moving poetry books in tribute of her father, include her poetry and prose as well as translated poems from the pen of her father, the poet, author and artist Zeev Kachel.

Uvi wrote and illustrated two children's books, *Jess and Wiggle* and *Now I Am Paper*. Watch the beautiful animations she created for these books on YouTube.

A Note to the Reader

Thank you for reading this book! I hope you enjoyed it. I invite you to check out more books from the same pen. There is always a new project on my drawing board, so come back to check it out.

I would love to hear what you thought of this book. You have the power of bringing it to the attention of more readers, by posting your own review. It would mean so much to me.

And another thing you can do to help me spread the word is this: please tell your friends about my work. How else will they hear about the story? How else will the characters, who sprang from my mind onto these pages, leap from there into new minds?

Bonus Excerpts
Excerpt: The White Piano

"Stop right there," I tell him. "It makes no sense to me! Why would she want to leave you right then, at the turning point of her life, when you could be there, by her side, fighting to hold her back, away from the brink?"

"This," says my father, "is something I, too, do not understand. Up to that point Natasha has changed, quietly, and grown so much stronger than me, to the point that, no matter how hard I tried, there was no pleasing her. Then she got word, somehow, about my moment of weakness: my fling, this little, one-night thing—that was all it was, back then—with Anita."

I look at him as if to say, Who cares about your moment of weakness? So far it has lasted ten years.

He looks away, saying, "Your mom, she was mad at me. She flared up in anger. It was painful. More painful than I had expected. Was she too proud to forgive me? Did she expect me to fight harder for her, so that she may take me back someday? There was no way to know. My God, she let me feel I was done, I was no longer needed."

"But, dad," I say, "did she believe she could face it alone, whatever *it* was? Was she willing to risk everything, and for what? For no better reason than pride?"

"God," he says. "I wish I knew."

"Enough," I say. "I don't want to hear it."

"That's just the thing, Ben. Natasha kept quiet, all these years, and so did I, for her sake. Gradually, her memory problems got worse and yet, no one knew: not our friends, not even her students, because she was so afraid, afraid to lose them. Teaching, for her, became more than a livelihood: it was the last token of her independence."

"You should have told me, dad."

"Well, how could I? There was no one here to whom I could talk."

"So, since then, has mom been diagnosed?"

"Well, son, it took a long time," he says, in a tired tone of voice, "Four years after she had left me, that was when they found out, at long last. And you, Ben, you were in Europe then, off to your medical studies, or something, with a light suitcase, and a heart heavy with anger, who knows why."

I want to say, Because I had to go, to be some place else. Because I had no family, with you cheating and mom throwing her wedding ring away. That's why. But without waiting for an explanation, my father moves on to say, "I just could not do it, could not bring myself to open up, to tell you about it."

Suddenly his voice trembles, and he wraps his arms around me, which makes me unsure if this is to lean on me—or perhaps, to protect me.

"Ben," he says, "this disease, unfortunately, it can strike in the prime of life. Natasha was forty-six when, after years of knowing that something was going terribly wrong, and not being able to put a finger on it, they finally diagnosed her."

"And," I hesitate to ask, "does it have a name?"

There is a sound by the entrance door, then a knock, once, twice, three times—but neither one of us moves. There is a somber expression on his face. His gaze is locked into mine, and something passes between us which I cannot express in words.

Meanwhile, between one knock and another there is a smaller sound: the click of the clock. Under the glass crystal, the black hand moves around the dial, from one minute mark to the next. It advances with a measured beat, the beat of loss, life, fear —until at long last, my father takes a long breath, and allows himself to say, "The doctors, they call it Early onset Familial Alzheimer's disease."

Then he passes by me on his way to open the door; which gives me a moment to think of mom.

I picture her staring at the black-and-white image of her brain, not quite understanding what they are telling her.

The doctors, they point out the overall loss of brain tissue, the enlargement of the ventricles, the abnormal clusters between nerve cells, some of which are already dying, shrouded eerily by a net of frayed, twisted strands. They tell her about the shriveling of the cortex, which controls brain functions such as remembering and planning.

And that is the moment when in a flash, mom can see clearly, in all shades of gray blooming there, on that image, how it happens, how her past and her future are slowly, irreversibly being wiped away—until she is a woman, forgotten.

Excerpt: The Music of Us

My son, Ben, has been gone for a month now, staying in some youth hostel in Rome. If I call him, if I stumble into revealing how scared I am that his mother is losing her mind, he may listen. He may heed my fears, grudgingly, and come back here, not even knowing how to offer his support to me. Should I ask for it?

The last thing I wish to do is lean on him for help. He is not strong enough, and whatever the problem may be with her, I can grit my teeth and handle it, somehow, all by myself. Besides, I pray for a spontaneous change in her. I mean, her memory may take a turn for the better just as quickly as it has deteriorated.

Given this hope I decide that for now I will not schedule the head X-Ray that her doctor recommended for her. I figure she has been through so many checkups, so many exams to rule out depression, vitamin B deficiency, and a long list of other possible ailments, all of which has been in vain.

So far, the results have failed to produce a conclusive diagnosis, and this new X-Ray will be no different, because from what I have read, Alzheimer's disease can be determined only through autopsy, by linking clinical measures with an examination of brain tissue. So this new medical hypothesis is just that: a hypothesis. One that cannot be proven; one that cannot go away. An ever-present threat.

Perhaps all she needs is rest. Time, I tell myself. I must give her time. Meanwhile I resolve to keep her condition secret from everyone, especially from my son. Let him enjoy his time away from home, his independence.

Since his departure I called him only once, three weeks ago, and said little, except for blurting out the mundane, "How's Rome?"

"Great," he said vaguely, adding no particulars.

I could not help myself from asking. "So, what about your plans?"

"What about them?"

"D'you have any?"

"For now I have none," he admitted, and immediately changed the subject. "How's mom?"

"Fine."

"Is she?"

"She is," I lied, hoping that the sound of my voice would not betray the tensing of my muscles, the tightening of my jaws.

"Oh good," he said. "Really, really good."

There is only one thing more difficult than talking to Ben, and that is writing to him. Amazingly, having to conceal what his mother is going through makes every word—even on subjects unrelated to her—that much harder. I find myself oppressed by my own self-imposed discipline, the discipline of silence.

And what can I tell him, really? That I keep digging into the past, mining its moments, trying to piece them together this way and that, dusting off each memory of Natasha, of how we were, the highs and lows of the music of us, to find out where the problem may have started?

To him, that may seem like an exercise in futility. For me, it is a necessary process of discovery, one that is as tormenting as it is delightful. If the dissonance in our life would fade away, so will the harmony.

Sometimes I go as far back as the moment we first met, when I was a soldier and she—a star, brilliant yet illusive. Natasha was a riddle to me then, and to this day, with all the changes she has gone through, she still is.

I often wonder: can we ever understand, truly understand each other—soldier and musician, man and woman, one heart and another? Will we ever again dance together to the same beat? Is there a point where we may still touch?

Excerpt: Dancing with Air

Overcome, suddenly, by exhaustion, Natasha stepped out of my embrace and plopped onto her suitcase. "Ma came to say goodbye, " she said. "I saw her across from me, as we left the shore. She was offering a prayer, tears running down her cheeks. Then, once out to sea, the Germans fired at us."

"Really? What happened?"

"The ships, they took up their positions in the convoy and plodded ahead. Straightaway, two of them were lost. One ran aground. The other, suffering from engine trouble, turned back to the harbor. And as for us I thought that was the end."

I shuddered at the thought.

"This journey," said Natasha, "it was more challenging than anything I've gone through in the past. Even watching Papa during his last months was easier, in a way, because back then I was on the outside, observing his pain."

I waited for her to continue.

After a slight reflection, she added, "I could only guess what was happening to him, I mean, the ways his illness drained his mind, the ways he suffered. But now, I wasn't an observer. I lived it, Lenny! Everyone on board—including me—was going through the same fear, the same hardship."

I could not help but ask her, "What were you thinking, putting yourself at risk?"

In reply, she rose to her feet. "For this very moment," she said, clinging to me, "I would go through it all over again."

I took a step back, to stress, "Your Mama, she's beside herself with worry, and as for me—"

"You talked to her?" asked Natasha, her eyes twinkling. "Of course you did, how else would you know to wait here for me? She doesn't get it—"

"And neither do I!"

"But Lenny, it's so simple! I missed you—"

"That's no reason, Natasha, for what you've done. Why leave home, especially now, when we're at war? If you love me, keep yourself safe, if only for my sake! Why, why put your life at risk —"

"Perhaps," she said, "I'm not looking for safety! Have you ever thought of that? Perhaps something else is more important to me."

"Like what?"

"I can't continue to depend on others, Lenny, the way I've done all my life. This is my time to change, to demand new things of myself, even if they happen to frighten me, even if I'm scared out of my mind."

"Not sure I understand—"

"Please try, Lenny."

"What is it you want?"

"Just this: to stop leaning on those closest to me."

"You could've done that back home, couldn't you?"

"That's the place where I'm being taken care of, to the point of feeling stuck. Worse than that: suffocated. Someone, usually Mama, drives me to where I need to be. Someone points me to the dressing room, calls me to the stage. I'm nothing more than a mechanical doll. All I do is respond."

"You do much more than that! You excite audiences, Natasha! And to me, you're an inspiration—"

"Yes, you admire the way I play, but in truth music is the only thing for which Papa trained me."

"You're too critical of yourself," I said.

To which she said, "No, Lenny. I've seen him decline, seen him lose his mind, and if—if, like him, I'll ever lose mine—how in the world will I recover? How will I find my way, when I've never developed the skill to do so?"

I lowered my head before her.

"Never," I said, "until now."

"Exactly," said Natasha. "Until now."

And a moment later, blotting the corner of her eye, where a tear was forming, she whispered to me, "Come closer, Lenny, snuggle up, but never, ever let me lean on you."

Excerpt: Rise to Power

To show respect, I fall to my knees before him. The floor is cold, having absorbed the damp of a long winter. The surface is porous, even crumbly here and there, cut of rocks from the Judea mountains. So is the surface of the stage, right in front of my eyes.

I cannot help noting the marks drawn by his spear in the film of dirt up there, around his boots. Scratch, twist, scratch again... No wonder he seems to be in such a royal pain: with all these attendants here to serve him, not a single one has managed to come up with the bright idea of sweeping the floor. They all carry weapons, but not one has a broom.

Sitting nearly immobile, Saul seems as chalky as the walls around him. He sits crumpled—in an odd way—upon the throne. His nails keep digging into the little velvety cushions that are stretched over the carved armrests. Not once does he give a nod in my direction, nor does he acknowledge my presence in any other way.

Which agitates me. It awakens my doubt, doubt in my skill. Much the same as I feel in my father's presence. Repressed. On the verge of acting out.

So, rising to my feet I blurt out, "Your majesty—"

"Don't talk," whispers one of the attendants. "Play."

I am pushed a step or two backwards, so as to maintain proper distance from the presence of the king. My name is called out in a clunky manner of introduction, after which I am instructed to choose from an array of musical instruments. I figure they must be the loot of war. So when I play them, the music of enemy tribes shall resound here, around the hall.

I pluck the strings of a sitar, then put it back down and pick up a lyre, which I make quiver, quiver with notes of fire! Then I rap, clap, tap, snap my fingers, and just to be cute, play a tune on my flute, after which I do a skip, skip, skip and a back flip. It is a long performance, and towards the end of it I find myself trying to catch my breath. Alas, my time is up. Even so I would not stop.

Entranced I go on to recite several of my poems, which I have never done before, for fear of exposing my most intimate, raw emotions, which is a risky thing for a man, and even riskier for a boy my age. Allowing your vulnerability to show takes one thing above all: a special kind of courage. Trust me, it takes balls.

So, having read the last verse I cast a look at the attendants, especially the ones closest to me. Their faces seem to have softened. I can sense them beginning to adore me. One of them comes over and taps my shoulder, which nearly knocks me off my feet. Another one laughs. Others wipe their eyes.

Then I glance at Saul, hoping for a tear, a smile, a word of encouragement. Instead I note an odd, vacant look on his face. Utter indifference. It stings me. Am I too short, too young, too curly for the role he has in mind for me?

Wiping the sweat off my brow I bow down before him and turn to leave the court, which is the moment he leans forward on his spear.

"Stop right there," says Saul. "Tell me: what can you do best?"

To which I say, "Recover."

He glowers at me as if to ask, Recover? From what?

"From this," I point out, daring to be honest. "Rejection."

Excerpt: Coma Confidential

Rhythms of footfalls are intensifying outside my hospital room. It must be morning. Immobile, all I can do is count beats. I must have spent days here—who knows, maybe even weeks—or else I wouldn't be able to tell time by means of listening to echoes.

It's a new skill, a new gain for me, barely significant enough to offset the loss of something far more important: my identity. Even so, I'm proud. I pat myself on the back. Mentally.

By their patter, I know that two pair of shoes have just stepped into the room. It doesn't take much to figure who is standing in them. The two nurses prattle about having to change my feeding tube. In a blink, a craving comes over me.

Oh, what I would give for a decent donut! I drool at the thought of dunking it into a bowl filled with smooth, warm, vanilla-flavored sugar glaze, then lifting it to my mouth for a quick lick.

One of the nurses wipes the dribble off my chin. I wish she would stop handling me. I wish I could turn my head away.

Meanwhile, my stomach is growling. I'm so hungry. At this point, never mind pastry. I'll take any real food—even peas and carrots, which normally I hate. Being able to chew them would cast me back among the living.

In this sorry state, I've come to acquire a new affinity with vegetables. Maybe they have feelings, too. Maybe they dread being poked about with a fork, just as much as I fear being injected. Maybe being sucked down that dark, cavernous windpipe to be consumed by something yet unknown is repulsive to them. I think that at long last, I understand carrots and peas. So no, I'm never going to put them in my mouth again.

Seriously, I prefer donuts.

"Oh my! Accident?" asks one nurse, while pumping liquid food into my stomach with a syringe.

"No, worse than that," says the other one. By comparison, her voice is lower and more mature. It is also secretive.

"What can be worse than an accident?"

"Don't even ask."

"Fine, then. Let's talk about something else."

"Like what?"

"Like, what d'you want to be, ten years from now?"

There's a faint sound—maybe the older nurse is scratching her head—which leaves the question unanswered. Oh, the things I'd say, if only I could revive my vocal cords! I'd shout, "Ten years, are you kidding me? Who cares! I just want to make it through today!"

But on second thought, I want more than that, much more. I strain my vocal cords in a desperate attempt to cry out, "I want to wake up from this nightmare, at the snap of my fingers. I want to walk away from this bed. Most of all, I want to know who I am. Is that too much to ask?"

Books by Uviart
Coma Confidential
(Volume I of *Ash Suspense Thrillers with a Dash of Romance*)
Kindle: B07L92YHST Paperback: 978-1791691592

Overkill
(Volume II of *Ash Suspense Thrillers with a Dash of Romance*)
Kindle: B084GDK156 Paperback: 979-8644328192

Overdose
(Volume III of *Ash Suspense Thrillers with a Dash of Romance*)
Kindle: B07VP4S6PK Paperback: 978-1086703665

Overdue
(Volume IV of *Ash Suspense Thrillers with a Dash of Romance*)
Kindle: B08S724T4G Paperback: 979-8599499671

Ash Suspense Thrillers: Trilogy

(Volume I-III of *Ash Suspense Thrillers with a Dash of Romance*)

Kindle: B0893MJNSY Paperback: 979-8648269644

Virtually Lace

(Volume I of *High-Tech Crime Solvers*)

Kindle: B07L968RXD Paperback: 978-1790407187

My Own Voice

(Volume I of *Still Life with Memories*)

Kindle: B013TA3FBS Paperback: 978-0984993215

The White Piano

(Volume II of *Still Life with Memories*)

Kindle: B013TAU7L4 Paperback: 978-1517049447

The Music of Us

(Volume III of *Still Life with Memories*)

Kindle: B013TCYWHC Paperback: 978-0-9849932-9-1

Dancing with Air

(Volume IV of *Still Life with Memories*)

Kindle: B01I4ENROY Paperback: 978-1536896534

Marriage before Death

(Volume V of *Still Life with Memories*)

Kindle: B0746NW5CD Paperback: 978-1974001736

Apart from Love

(*Still Life with Memories Bundle I*)

Kindle: B006WPITP0 Paperback: 978-0-9849932-0-8

Apart from War

(*Still Life with Memories Bundle II*)

Kindle: B07MMZLD7Z Paperback: 978-1792131592

Rise to Power

(Volume I of *The David Chronicles*)

Kindle: B00H6PMZ0U Paperback: 978-0-9849932-4-6

A Peek at Bathsheba

(Volume II of *The David Chronicles*)

Kindle: B00LEPPDV6 Paperback: 978-0-9849932-7-7

The Edge of Revolt

(Volume III of *The David Chronicles*)

Kindle: B00Q5WVKA6 Paperback: 978-0984993284

The David Chronicles: Trilogy

(Volume I-III of *The David Chronicles*)

Kindle: B00QYGF6WG Paperback: 978-1797440699

The David Chronicles: Art

(Volume IV-XI of *The David Chronicles*)

Kindle: B08YWSH7HC Paperback: 979-8721612886

Inspired by Art: Fighting Goliath

(Art book. Volume IV of *The David Chronicles*)

Kindle: B01MSBNSE4   Paperback 978-1797726212

Inspired by Art: Fall of a Giant

(Art book. Volume V of *The David Chronicles*)

Kindle: B01MSBS82Q   Paperback: 978-1092307765

Inspired by Art: Rise to Power

(Art book. Volume VI of *The David Chronicles*)

Kindle: B01N2786VX   Paperback: 978-1092263207

Inspired by Art: A Peek at Bathsheba

(Art book. Volume VII of *The David Chronicles*)

Kindle: B01MUFS9OA   Paperback: 978-1092306225

Inspired by Art: The Edge of Revolt

(Art book. Volume VIII of *The David Chronicles*)

Kindle: B01N6ZG0W8 Paperback: 978-1091306158

Inspired by Art: The Last Concubine

(Art book. Volume IX of *The David Chronicles*)

Kindle: B01N2AXQP2 Paperback: 978-1092302715

A Favorite Son

Kindle: B00AUZ3LGU Paperback: 978-0-9849932-5-3

Twisted

Kindle: B00D7Q3IY4

Paperback: 978-0984993260 Nook: 2940151689588

Home

Kindle: B00960TE3Y

Paperback: 978-09849932-3-9 Nook: 2940151729468

Can We Still Love

(Poetry)

Kindle: B0GV3G23V4 Paperback: B0GY8Q1Y9Z

Virtually Yummy: Recipes that Inspire

(Cookbook)

Kindle: B085BDNDM5 Nook: 2940163988655

Apple: id1501182051 Kobo: 9781393589853

בית

(Poetry in Hebrew)
Paperback: 978-1494920968 Nook: 1127367962
Apple: id1302908918 Kobo: 9781540199966

Jess and Wiggle

Kindle: B013D1W0SM Paperback: 978-1494920968

Now I Am Paper

Kindle: B00YQS4O72 Paperback: 978-1494919429